SIDESWIPED

JC RYAN

SIDESWIPED

JC RYAN

vinci
BOOKS

By JC Ryan

Rex Dalton K9 Thrillers

The Fulcrum
The Power of Three
Unchained
Sideswiped
The Inca Con
The French Girl
Duty of Care
Donna Teresa
Under the Pope's Windows
The Shanghai Strain
The Delphi Technique
Holes in the Wall
The Abyss
Unearthed
Remorseless
The Message

Dedicated to my good friend Mitch Pender, a military dog trainer, for giving me the idea for this series and guiding me through the intricate and amazing capabilities and psychology of those majestic four-legged soldiers.
Mitch has a lifetime of experience and exceptional depth of knowledge as a military dog handler and trainer.

Vinci Books

vinci-books.com

Published by Vinci Books Ltd in 2025

1

About Sideswiped

Rex and Digger had to get out of India in a hurry. They arrive in Thailand and shortly after Rex meets a beautiful girl, Sunstra and before long there is a romance in the making. But then Sunstra disappears when a tsunami devastates the southern part of the country.

While Rex and Digger try to find her, her family receives a ransom demand. She is alive but she's not going to remain alive for long if her father doesn't sign the papers to sell his land.

Rex and Digger have to race against time to rescue her before she is killed.

Chapter One

Bangkok, Thailand. Present time

"So, Ruan, you bought this tuk-tuk just so you could let your dog ride with you? Why not just get a small car?" Sunstra Chevapravatgumrong, Rex Dalton's Thai language teacher asked.

"A car in this crazy traffic? Nah, that I'll never do to myself," Rex answered with a smile.

It was their first outing, not a date, because of the language school's policy against fraternization between students and teachers. Rex, always a bit of a rebel, especially when it came to red tape, neatly circumvented the policy by not asking her out on a date, but asking her to give him a guided tour of Bangkok, so he could improve his knowledge of the Thai language and culture—two birds with one stone, or in this case, three, because the outing gave him the chance to also get to know her better, which had been his main objective from the outset.

Using his Ruan Daniel nom de guerre, Rex had been in

Thailand for a little over a month. His trip to Thailand had a twofold purpose. The first was to investigate cosmetic surgery options, and the second was part of his new life-goal to explore historical sites across the world and soak up cultures new to him, as well as adding new languages to his already impressive repertoire.

However, getting around Bangkok with his big Dutch shepherd dog, Digger, had been more problematical than he'd expected.

Even getting into the country with him had been a hassle. Digger had been given a clean bill of health by his vet in India, but for reasons of anonymity, Rex had skipped the step of getting a government seal on the paperwork, leery of having his own papers examined too closely or questions about how Digger had been brought into India in the first place. The honest answer to *that* question, if asked, would have been illegally, not to mention that Rex had also entered India illegally. So, Rex thought it best to just let the seal slide, and thus far he'd gotten away with it.

Except then, upon arrival in Thailand, he'd found himself in a lengthy argument with a Thai official over the lack of a seal on Digger's papers. The back and forth between Rex and the official went on for so long, had Digger been a four-year-old boy instead of a dog, he would have been dancing around with both hands on his privates, anxious to find a bathroom before he had an embarrassing accident right there on the carpet of the official's office. Rex had paid a 'fine' of one-thousand bhat, about thirty US dollars, to have the matter dealt with expediently. That was Rex's first palm-greasing experience in Thailand, but there were going to be many more.

Further hassles were that no means of public transportation would allow Digger to board, notwithstanding his palm-greasing offers, so he'd been spending a fortune on taxis and tuk-tuks. Naturally, every driver had seen him coming and used the opportunity to charge him double, even after fierce negotiation, because of Digger. Without Digger, they'd have had less leverage. Even though he was clearly *farang*, a foreigner, Rex's experience in bargaining gained in the Middle East was strong enough to overcome their initial attempts to scam him. But they'd apparently banded together over the question of taking dogs onboard, and after he'd waved three or four off, he still couldn't get a lower price.

It wasn't the money so much as his knowledge that foreigners paying more inconvenienced locals, who couldn't get needed transportation when more lucrative tourists were around, willing to pay the higher price either through ignorance or because it was still cheaper than at home. The whole concept went against his grain and he didn't want to contribute to that.

Neither did he want to be scammed. After the third time it happened in the first couple of days, he'd had enough. There was only one answer – buy his own tuk-tuk. That hadn't proved easy either, as tuk-tuks were classed as work vehicles, and his visa didn't permit him to work. Another round of negotiations with government officials, a few one-thousand-bhat incentives, and a few inquiries later, he was the proud owner of a used tuk-tuk, licensed for private use only. So now he and Digger had their own hassle-free ride, and there was even enough space for a passenger, maybe two if they were prepared to squash themselves a bit.

He'd taken a month-to-month lease on an apartment in an older building for the same reason. He could have afforded a modern building with all sorts of modern amenities, but most of them weren't dog-friendly, even though the people in general were. Those who would usually allow dogs were horrified at Digger's size. They preferred dogs that could be taken through the lobby in carriers, or preferably peeking cutely out of a lady's oversized handbag. Not sixty-five-pound black Dutch shepherds.

Nevertheless, because Rex intended to spend several weeks in Thailand, he'd finally found one that had a pleasant view and a few amenities, like a gym and swimming pool, which were well-kept, though not very modern.

If Digger had anything to say about the accommodations, he kept it to himself. At the moment, he was smiling widely, his tongue lolling out of one side of his broad open mouth, looking around as if he thought he was being chauffeured around the city on his own sightseeing tour. He occupied most of the back seat of the tuk-tuk, with Sunstra next to Rex in front.

Rex only cared about his growing attraction to the beautiful Thai woman. He was listening closely to her explanation, in Thai as he'd requested, about the long, unpronounceable Thai surnames. Unlike Western cultures, where surnames often referred to long-forgotten relatives, an occupation, or a region from which the family originated, Thai culture had not commonly used surnames before 1913, when the Surname Act came into effect and dictated that surnames must be adopted.

"But why did they adopt such long ones?" he asked. "Wouldn't that have been the ideal opportunity to choose an easy short surname such as Ng or Ling, or Smith or…"

"Wait, I'm not finished. In the original Surname Act, there was also a provision that Thais of Chinese descent would use their original Chinese names, with the prefix Sae. But later, nationalism meant that some of them felt discrimination. Does that make sense?"

"Sure. Like times in the US when various nationalities were unpopular. Irish in the mid-eighteen-hundreds. Germans and Japanese after World War II, and so on."

"Mexicans now?" she inquired with a wry smile.

"Well, we call them Latinos or Hispanics, but yeah. Not only those from Mexico, but anyone with a Spanish last name sometimes. But that doesn't explain your long names."

"Well, what happened was they began to translate the Chinese name into Thai, but by that time, someone creating a new Thai name because they couldn't duplicate any had to add decorative words to the meaning. The names got longer and longer until 1965, when the Persons Act came into effect and put a limit of ten Thai letters, excluding vowels and diacritical marks. But that still allows for quite long names. And the ability to change one's surname with permission from the head of the family exacerbates the situation."

"Why would anyone do that? Change their surname, I mean," Rex asked, rather disingenuously, since he personally had several identities.

"Mostly because of separation or divorce, but oftentimes people do it to change bad luck," she said.

Rex had a near-eidetic memory, but he had to make a special effort to remember the mouthful of eighteen characters in Sunstra's surname. Remembering his Thai lessons, he carefully pronounced it when he said, "*Khun* Chevapra-vatgumrong, would you care to stop and get a bite to eat?"

Sunstra, he'd learned, meant 'girl with beautiful eyes'. He'd never heard a more apt name, as her almond-shaped eyes were expressive and large, but only large enough to perfectly balance her oval-shaped face. Long, dark-brown hair framed her porcelain skin, and her eyes were a color between brown and gray that fascinated him. He'd seen them change from warm brown to stormy gray depending on what she was wearing or her mood. She lined them with dark pencil and thickened the lashes with mascara. Though he'd never preferred make-up to a woman's natural look, he was happy to make an exception in Sunstra's case as he had to admit it added to the mystery of those profound eyes.

A thin, straight nose and full lips, today wearing a bright scarlet lipstick completed her appearance and added up to exquisite beauty.

Her beautiful eyes sparkled as her silvery laugh delighted his ears. "You don't need to address me so formally, Ruan. We prefer first names, and even if you call me *khun*, you don't need to add my surname. It's like your 'miss' or 'mister'," she continued, pronouncing the English words with an accent that made them sound like mees and meester. "Except that you may address anyone of either sex with just the one word."

"Then in that case, *Khun* Sunstra, would you care for something to eat?"

She laughed and shook her head again, which he interpreted to mean no, until she said, "I can see you will need much more tutoring before I can turn you loose in this country. Yes, I would love to have a meal with you."

Rex grinned. *Much more tutoring is exactly what I have in mind.*

After a pleasant evening of conversation and exquisite Thai cuisine, Rex delivered Sunstra to her small home near the language school where they'd met. He kissed her goodnight on the cheek, receiving another knee-buckling smile for his efforts. But just then, when he kissed her, Digger moved between them and nudged Rex away. He yawned, letting out a squeak that Rex had never heard before. He glanced at the dog, noticed he didn't seem happy, and decided to ignore the signal, since there didn't seem to be any immediate danger or any other reason to be unhappy.

He was tempted to immediately set up the next outing with her, but mindful of the school's policy, he refrained. It didn't have to do with the power exchange between a teen and an authority figure, as it would have in the US. As nearly as he could figure, it was about favoritism.

Only two more weeks and I don't have to worry about the policy anymore. Maybe I can hire her as my personal tutor then.

Walking back to the street after seeing her safely inside, he turned to Digger. "What was that about, buddy?"

Digger uttered a soft *woof* that Rex couldn't interpret, but that didn't keep him from ending the conversation on his terms.

"Well, don't do it again. Those are important moments in any relationship between a man and a woman. Something I'm sure dogs know nothing about."

Digger ignored him and looked away without answering.

Chapter Two

Agra, India. Five weeks ago

Rex and Digger were strolling on the grounds of the Taj Mahal after Rex paid an exorbitant sum to an official to have a large "Service Dog" sandwich board attached to Digger's harness. Rex suspected it was unofficial, but so far no one had hassled them. Digger didn't mind being on leash. He was used to it.

Of course, Digger wasn't a service dog, but that was the ruse Rex had used ever since inheriting the dog from his friend, Trevor Madigan, a former SAS operative from Australia, who'd been killed in an ambush in Afghanistan. Digger, an Australian military dog, had been his companion since Trevor asked Rex to take care of him with his dying breath. Rex, mortally scared of dogs since he'd been attacked by one as a small child, had agreed. There was no way he was going to deny his friend's deathbed request.

The two of them, Rex and Digger, at best had what could be called a strained relationship while Trevor was still alive. That was mainly due to Rex's fear of dogs, which he never told anyone about, but was obviously sensed by Digger who badgered him about it.

But since Rex was a man of his word, he and Digger worked through their issues, and as it turned out, Digger had trained him to relax around dogs, had acknowledged him as his alpha in their pack of two, and was incredibly useful in a scrape. He also did a great impersonation of a service dog. Over time they'd become inseparable mates.

It had been a month since the interruption of his new life as a globe-trotting student of history had ended with Rex acquiring an Indian IT specialist as his personal assistant. He'd then indulged his desire to see more of the historical sites of India, with the knowledge that his former life as a black ops government sanctioned assassin was no longer open to him since the ambush that led to the deaths of his entire team, including Trevor Madigan. Afterward, with Digger's help, he'd pursued the people responsible for the ambush and discovered who'd betrayed him. He dealt with some of them, but there were some still on his blacklist, to be dealt with at a time of his choosing. He'd escaped Afghanistan with Digger, a bundle of cash, a small fortune in diamonds, and a stack of computer hard drives containing valuable information about the main players involved in the drug trade of Afghanistan, including those in the US ultimately responsible for the betrayal and killing of Rex's men. He was convinced the latter also contained enough information about the drug lord's secret bank accounts to allow him to help himself to a major fortune.

The Taj Mahal was one of the last sites on his list to visit in India. One of the seven wonders of the modern world, meaning "Crown of the Palace", the elegant edifice is an ivory-white marble mausoleum on the south bank of the

Yamuna river in the Indian city of Agra. The Mughal emperor Shah Jahan, who reigned from 1628 to 1658, erected it to house the tomb of his favorite wife. Centered in formal gardens, the majesty of the white marble structure was breathtaking. So much so that Rex's carefully-constructed identity had a near-miss in the next moment.

All Rex's appearance at the time needed to simulate being blind was a white stick. He was wearing a big hat against the mid-day sun and sunglasses to protect him from the brightness of the sparkling white marble of the palace. Digger on a leash beside him, with the prominent Service Dog sign, completed the subterfuge, though that hadn't been on Rex's mind when he set out that morning.

Nonetheless, it quickly became very much on his mind when he almost bumped right into someone from his past. Josh Farley. And with him was a woman Rex didn't know. Not surprising that he didn't know her, as when he and Josh had been acquainted there were no women in the picture. All this flashed through his mind as he surreptitiously backed off and tried to calm his jangled nerves.

That could have been a disaster!

As he let Josh and the woman gain ground while he dropped back, Rex's mind raced even as he tried to regulate his heart rate and breathing.

What the hell is Josh doing here? Holiday? Who is the woman with him? Maybe his girlfriend? Wife? Nah can't be.

He knew Josh well enough – Josh had been recruited into CRC, a highly secret black ops paramilitary organization for whom Rex had been a top agent, a few years after Rex. Rex had given him some training, and he was good. One tough, lean, mean bastard. CRC agents didn't have time for a wife, not while they were still young enough to be in the field. Last time he saw Josh he didn't even have a girlfriend.

But most important of all, what was he doing here, and who was that woman with him? Rex had the perturbation that it might have something to do with him.

Were they looking for him, or were they on some other mission? Or were they on holiday? From what he'd observed in the short time since recognizing Josh, there was nothing in their behavior that gave Rex any indication they weren't simply tourists, just like the thousands of others there. But then, posing as a couple was a typical cover story for agents working together.

And since when did CRC have female agents, if indeed that's who that woman is?

He didn't have a good feeling about it. He dropped further behind. Nobody with something to hide likes coincidence. Cops, spooks, soldiers, military analysts, and many others don't believe in it, and neither did Rex. No wonder one of his favorite quotes about it immediately came to mind.

Coincidence is the word we use when we can't see the levers and pulleys- Emma Bull

Rex knew intellectually that coincidence did happen— on occasion. Even so, the last thing he wanted was to be coincidentally or deliberately or in any other manner recognized by anyone he knew before his 'death'.

In the aftermath of the explosion that killed his team, wracked with grief and rage over the senseless deaths of Trevor and the rest of the team, Rex had gone on a vengeful spree, killing those he discovered were immediately responsible. He'd left a swath of death and destruction that would have pointed straight to him, if he hadn't decided to disappear and be 'dead' in order to stay alive.

Another consideration was that although he knew who the US kingpin was, he still wasn't sure if John Brandt, known as the 'Old Man', the CEO of CRC was one of those responsible. But his order to raid the house where the tragedy occurred had come from Brandt. Rex couldn't discount the possibility. Knowing he needed time and space to get his head back on straight, he'd decided that, since he was no doubt assumed dead, he'd just stay that way, use the resources he'd gained in punishing the local perpetrators, and for the foreseeable future follow the interests he'd had as a kid and later in college.

Accordingly, he'd sneaked over Afghanistan's border into Pakistan, over Pakistan's into India, and begun to use those financial resources to build a cover and a new life. The threat to that new life represented by Josh Farley and whoever the woman was could throw a monkey wrench in the works, which he would not allow to happen.

Overcoming the initial adrenaline rush, Rex sped up to within a couple yards of Josh and his friend to observe them more closely. He now felt there was no worry that they'd detect his presence for a couple of reasons. The first was that there were thousands of tourists around them. Seeing someone more than once was almost guaranteed by the press of the crowds, since it would be difficult to go against the flow.

The other was that Digger was with him. Josh would have no reason to look for Rex in the company of a dog. Even though he'd never shared his fear of dogs with anyone, no one from CRC had ever seen him in the company of one. Digger's presence was the perfect cover, despite standing out as a rarity in the complex.

Rex and Digger followed the two for an hour or so, wending their way slowly up to the entrance of the tomb with the rest of the crowd, who were staying more or less in the same order as when they'd entered the grounds. Despite his official service dog status, Digger wouldn't be allowed inside, and Rex would not leave him on his own outside. He needed to try to figure out what Josh and the woman were doing here before they reached the entrance.

Within half an hour, he'd decided they weren't a couple, well, at least not a new one. They didn't hold hands, steal a kiss, or appear keen for each other like new couples would. And this woman was eye-candy. Josh would have every reason to not keep his hands off her if they were a couple. No, from his perspective, they looked and interacted more like partners.

So, then they must be on a mission. What else could it be? They did obviously know each other, as they spoke back and forth. To Rex the most logical and safest conclusion was that they were looking for him, though he couldn't imagine how they'd determined he'd be in India.

Am I just being paranoid?

No sooner had he asked himself the question when the mental retort came. *Better to be paranoid and alive than not paranoid and dead.*

The only reason for CRC to send agents to find him would be to apprehend or kill him.

Probably the latter, since it had already been tried once.

And if he was right that they were looking for him, then it meant that 'they', in the person of John Brandt, knew he was alive and even where he'd gone.

How could he have found out?

It occurred to him, not for the first time, that a thorough forensic search of the explosion site would find his DNA lacking. He could only hope that they didn't know about Digger. Neither Josh nor the woman gave any indication while Rex followed them that they particularly noticed the big, black dog.

Rex was still ruminating on the probability that Josh and the woman were looking for him when they reached the front of the line and disappeared into the mausoleum. He'd get no further opportunity for observation without the risk of coming face-to-face with them, so he turned back, wading against the flow of foot traffic, toward the exit where he could wait and hope to pick up their trail again later.

While he waited, partially concealed, he analyzed his situation. Rex was fully aware that his training with CRC would be with him forever. Even though it had been more than a month since he'd been involved in an operation, he certainly hadn't lost his edge. He still had all the sharpness of a highly intelligent paramilitary operator with field craft prowess second to none, making him worthy of the names his enemies gave him—*El Gato*, the cat, *Alshaytan*, The Devil, or the Ghost—though they never knew his real identity.

He still had his hatred for terrorists and any activity that fueled their agenda, including illicit drug and arms dealers. And he didn't know whether Josh, or anyone else at CRC, or just John Brandt had been instrumental in the ambush that severed him from his former life. But he intended to find out when he could assure his own survival.

So, what to do now?

He had no doubt he could take Josh, the woman, or both and interrogate them. But then what? Whether they were there to find him, or he'd been mistaken, he'd have to kill them to protect his anonymity. But Rex was not a ruthless killer. The people he'd killed before had given ample reason to meet such a fate. Killing one or both Josh and the woman would go against his grain, and it would be a sure way to let Brandt know he was alive—as surely as if he let them live and allowed them to report back. Not only that, it would unleash the wrath of all CRC agents, and who knew how many agents from other security agencies? After all, the woman could be Mossad, or MI6 or another intelligence agency for all he knew. Rex was confident about his abilities, and that meant he knew his own limits.

Rex had trained Josh himself in hand-to-hand combat and in street craft and knew what he was capable of. He hadn't worried about Josh or the woman noticing Digger in the queue for entrance to the Taj Mahal, but if either had and then saw him again in a different context, they'd be instantly alerted they were being followed. He'd have to 'park' Digger somewhere, and then he'd be at a disadvantage in a fight, with two of them to subdue without killing them before he could question them.

After thinking it all through, it seemed bugging out was the better part of valor after all.

"Come on, Digger. This country has become unsafe for the two of us. We need to get out of here and find somewhere we can go to change my appearance."

Chapter Three

Mumbai, India

Rex had a few sites left on his list of those to see before he left India, but the encounter with Josh and the unknown woman had brought up something he had been thinking of on and off since walking off the reservation in Afghanistan —cosmetic surgery.

But he kept on kicking that can down the road and never did the research or got the professional advice he needed for his decision. Now it was clear he'd potentially left that and some other important business unattended for too long.

One of the considerations arguing against a major transformation was the fact that after he'd had occasion to spread his cash among several bank accounts, he'd had several sets of fake IDs made – one for each bank account. And Digger had papers to identify him as the service dog of each of the identities.

He'd obtained the first ID, the one that said he was

Ruan Daniel, as soon as he'd been able after leaving Afghanistan. It had helped to facilitate traveling to Saudi Arabia and rescuing the daughter of a wonderful old couple, whom he'd met by chance. That daughter, Rehka Gyan, was now his IT chief in a barely-formed idea of an enterprise to help victims of bad guys whom he relieved of their money. The Saudi excursion had been costly, dangerous, and extremely satisfying. It not only saved Rehka and a few of her fellow harem 'pleasure wives' from a terrible life but had also satisfied his need for action and provided the means for those women to live financially independent for the rest of their lives.

The bottom line was he now had several sets of expensive paper that would be rendered useless with a change in appearance that was much different from what was on those papers. Rex had enough money to provide for him and Digger for a very long time and to create new IDs for both of them if he decided to do so. The problem was finding reputable forgers.

In the days leading up to Rehka's rescue, Rex had made a friend in Mumbai, who, because he was a policeman, could refer him to slick operators in the seedy underworld of the city. Those that the police knew were dirty but couldn't pin a crime on or who they only kept a watch on so that they could rather go after the bigger fish—the forger's clients. In fact, it was this friend, Aarav Patel, who'd referred him to each of the various forgers he'd used, as Rex didn't ever want to use the same one. Aarav owed Rex his life, and because he'd seen that Rex's methods, though not legal at all, produced results the police wanted but couldn't, he conveniently never asked questions whenever Rex came to him with a new request.

Therefore, Aarav wouldn't be surprised when Rex asked

him for the name of an honest diamond appraiser and those of a few reputable diamond dealers. He wouldn't bother to ask why—he'd assume Rex had some that he wanted to sell or maybe he wanted to buy some—he wouldn't ask.

True to Rex's assumption, Aarav supplied the names and then went about his own business without asking questions. Rex went straight to the appraiser and had those diamonds he'd taken from Rehka's former captor valued before he approached the dealers. They were worth about two-hundred thousand US dollars, he found. If he had them cut and polished, they'd be worth more.

However, Rex had no time for that. He needed to be out of India fast. The fact he'd bumped into someone he knew amid over a billion people told him it was no coincidence, and if they could find him once, they could find him again. Next time, he might not be so lucky as to see them before they saw him.

By the end of his first day back in Mumbai, he knew the worth of his holdings, but it was too late in the day to have the diamonds converted to cash. He also had another task. Rex returned to his hotel with his diamonds, placed them in the room safe, and turned on his laptop. It was time to research the best place to go for cosmetic surgery.

Like many Americans, Rex would have preferred any surgery to be done in the US. Unlike most, he didn't have that option. There was no way he could enter the US in the wake of 9-11 and expect it to remain a secret. For all he knew, his handsome mug was on a watch list—he would've been surprised if it wasn't. Therefore, his requirements, in order of priority, was non-US, considered safe and up to date, and preferably nearby. The last was because he assumed countries in Europe where he could go would be cooperating with US agencies and would also be on the lookout for him.

That still left quite a few choices in the Middle East and Asia. He had no desire to return to the Middle East. Southeast Asia it was. After doing further research, he decided on Thailand, not only because it enjoyed a reputation as a good destination for medical tourism, but because it was an area rich in history and culture. Besides, he could learn Thai while he was there, bringing his repertoire to seven languages: French, Spanish, German, Italian, Arabic, a working knowledge of Mandarin, and finally fluency in Thai if he stayed a few months.

"Okay, Digger, we're going to Thailand," he announced. Digger lifted his ears at the sound of his name but had no comment about the destination. If his facial expression could be interpreted it would probably have been something along the lines of, "So, when are we going?" or "What are we waiting for?"

The next morning, Rex made the rounds with one-third of his diamonds, placing the rest in safety deposit boxes among his bank accounts first and collecting some of the cash stashed in them. After visiting five of the diamond dealers, he had $150,000 in cash, which he would redistribute in the bank accounts a little at a time, little enough to avoid suspicion, to join the approximately $200,000 he had taken from his Afghanistan exploits and had already deposited to his various accounts.

It would have made a lesser man or any accountant's head swim, but Rex easily kept track of his assets. Between his near-eidetic memory and the necessity for survival, he'd never forgotten anything essential.

That night, he booked a flight to Thailand online for the following morning. He had two more errands to do before he left. The first was to visit Rehka and inspect her progress in setting up what they'd discussed – the trust account for her and the other women he'd rescued from Saudi Arabia, and a secure means of communication between the two of them in the future. The second was to dispose of his van, and he knew exactly what he wanted to do with it.

After accomplishing his first errand and saying goodbye to Rehka just before sunrise the next morning, he visited Aarav Patel at home. His friend was surprised to see him so early, but graciously invited him to enter. Rex declined, explaining he had a flight to catch.

Aarav's jaw dropped in astonishment when Rex handed him the keys to the van.

"My friend, your family is growing. You need this vehicle and I don't. Please accept it as a gift."

Aarav's face clouded. "Ruan, I can't accept this. It looks too much like a bribe for all my favors to you."

"I can't remember any favors you did for me. What are you talking about?" Rex was grinning. "But let's not get hung up on details and facts. Let me speak to your wife."

Just then, Aarav's wife came to the door and asked why they were standing at the door instead of inside, where she had breakfast ready to serve. Rex took advantage of the situation and repeated what he'd said to Aarav to begin with.

By then, the children were awake and tumbled out the door to give Digger hugs. Aarav gave Rex a desperate look and tried to herd his kids back inside before they woke the neighbors. Rex just grinned and dropped the key into Aarav's wife's hands.

"I'll see you again, my friend," he promised.

He walked away and used his cell phone to hail a cab.

Next stop: Thailand.

Chapter Four

Josh Farley and Marissa Bisset were having what she called a vigorous discussion. Marissa was ready to throw in the towel.

"It's impossible to even start looking for someone in this country," she said. "There are too many people, and it isn't as if we'll just bump into him. We don't even know for certain he's here."

"We don't know he isn't," Josh countered.

She knew he wouldn't want to let the Old Man down, and he had told her already he wasn't going back without something to report. Now he repeated it as his mantra. "I'm not going back…"

"Without something to report," she snapped. "I know. You've said that every day since we got here. Well, I say we have something to report. We didn't find him, and the trail is not just cold. We never had a trail to follow in the first place. End of story."

"But listen, we haven't covered all the ground."

"Are you serious?" she half-shouted. "Over a billion people! Hello!"

"No, that isn't what I mean. Remember, we know he got away with a lot of cash and some diamonds, from that guy Usama, right?"

"Wrong. We *think* he's the one who raided Usama's compound and emptied the safes. We have no way of knowing." She dropped her head in her hands and muttered through her mane of nearly black hair, "It's a fool's game. Brandt is delusional."

Josh jumped to their boss's defense immediately. It was one of the things she found endearing about the younger agent. At twenty-five, he still believed the good guys always won. Even though CRC had a remarkable record, Marissa knew they didn't *always* win. Sometimes she wasn't even certain they were always the good guys. This boondoggle could be one of the times they didn't win, but she didn't really want to argue with Josh.

The truth was, she'd grown a little too fond of Josh. Even though he was young and, in her view, a little naïve, there was no question he was good at what he did. So, when he hotly defended Brandt, she didn't tell him that at ten years his senior, she had a better grasp on reality. Instead, she sighed and asked what he thought their next move should be.

"We haven't run into him at any of the places we thought he might have gone, given his interest in history. We could have just missed him, right? I mean, we were at one place when he was somewhere else. I think we have to play the odds. How likely is it that someone else went after the guy who set up that ambush within a few hours of it happening? We, and that includes you, are in an industry where we can't afford to believe in coincidence. But we, you

22

and I, know that coincidence is also real. In this case we are not staking our lives on it, so why not keep on going for a while longer and see if coincidence smiles upon us?"

All right. If he's going to play the Socratic method, I can go along.

"Admittedly, not likely. It was probably a survivor, but what makes you think it was Rex?"

"It's just a hunch, and one The Old Man shares. So, it isn't likely it was anyone else. And we have the reports from people who should know that Usama's safes were full of cash and diamonds. Don't forget, whoever it was also took the computer hard drives."

Marissa tilted her head. "Why is that significant?"

"Because it tells us something about what the person's intentions were. If he'd meant to stay in the area, he'd have taken the computers. He needed to travel light, which tells me he meant to leave the country."

Not bad. I didn't think of that.

"That still doesn't pin it to Rex. Anyone who did that would have wanted to put distance between himself and the scene of the crime. But, be that as it may, let's say you're right. He's got diamonds, a wad of cash, and three or four hard drives from Usama's computers. How does that tell us where he's going?"

Josh grinned, and Marissa realized he thought he had her buy-in. What he had was her interest, but it wouldn't hurt to play along. Only now *she* was Socrates. She waited for his answer, which was clearly on the tip of his tongue. She didn't know what he was waiting for.

"I'd tell you, but then..."

Oh, no, you're not playing that game with me!

Marissa leaped at him, knocked him onto his back on the bed where he'd been sitting, and straddled his chest. "You'd have to what?" She laughed, but the next moment she found herself flat on her own back, Josh pinning her to the bed and grasping her wrists, her arms over her head.

"Get off me, and don't get any ideas either!" she exclaimed in a mock serious tone.

He let go of her wrists and rolled off her. "Just needed to get your attention, *Mrs. Farley*." They'd been posing as a couple despite their age difference, which was impossible to see. Josh was a pleasant-faced, All-American type. Not movie-star handsome, but he looked slightly older than he was. Marissa, on the other hand, looked quite a bit younger than she was, with the effect that it looked as if they were of the same age. Besides that, her beauty would be the focus of anyone looking at them as a couple in any event. If anyone were to find out that Josh was so much younger, they'd probably assume he was wealthy and she a trophy wife.

"Don't ever do that again," she said.

"You started it," he retorted.

She began to laugh. He joined in, standing and then extending his hand to help her up from her awkward position.

"Okay, I plead guilty. Let's focus. Let's assume Rex is the person who killed Usama and relieved him of his belongings, that he has a wad of cash and some diamonds that he left the country with because he was traveling light, and that he came here. Why did he come here?" she asked.

"Easy. India's the world's diamond capital. He's planning to sell them here." Josh, still standing and now looking down at her as she remained seated on the bed, crossed his arms as if that were the end of it.

"How do you figure that?" she said. "I thought Brussels in Belgium was the diamond capital."

"Here's the thing, though," he said. "Where did he get

the diamonds? The drug lord he took them from, assuming it was him…"

She nodded. "We're out of luck if we *don't* assume it was Rex who killed him. Consider that a given."

"Okay. So, my point is, they were likely as dirty as their previous owner. He can't sell them in Belgium, where every diamond is tracked according to source. But in India, specifically in Surat, it's wide-open by design. They're working on illicitly mined stones right alongside legitimate ones. Where else is he going to peddle stolen stones? Especially stolen conflict diamonds, which is most likely what Usama had. By the time they've been cut and polished in Surat, no one would be able to figure out where they came from, just like all the other illicit stones on the market. Occam's Razor."

"Wait a minute. In the first place, you can't cite Occam's Razor when we've made a ton of assumptions. And you might have a point, but you also have some faulty conclusions. He's got diamonds, but he's also got cash. Quite a bit of it. How do we know he plans to sell the diamonds or that he hasn't sold them already?"

Josh looked crestfallen, then brightened. "Because, if he doesn't, then he'd have probably gone somewhere else. Or maybe…"

"Don't waste your breath to even try to make sense of what you just said. I agree, we've got to start somewhere, and as you pointed out, Brandt thinks he'd have come here, too. So if we're going to continue this wild-goose-chase, what's our next move?"

"I say we go to Surat and question diamond dealers," Josh said.

"Okay, but let's just do a bit of research about what that would mean."

They got on their laptops and began searching for information about Surat and the diamond industry there, and were soon depressed to learn that Surat was not only one of the world's fastest-growing cities, with five million residents and growing, but also that half a million of them were involved in some way in the diamond trade. Inside the countless rows of crumbling, whitewashed, concrete office buildings, teeming masses were cutting, polishing, or moving stones.

They didn't have to say it, but the facts spoke for themselves—it was as hopeless a task as running into Rex at a tourist site by coincidence.

Now that she was mildly invested in the outcome again, Marissa wondered, "What else would he be doing besides selling his diamonds?"

Josh heard and snapped his fingers. "False ID!" he crowed. "He'd need a passport, a legend, maybe more than one."

"Good idea, but…" Marissa almost didn't want to say it and start the argument all over again.

"But what?"

"How are we going to find the forgers who created those IDs for him? It's not as if we can place an ad in the newspaper and ask them to contact us."

"Marissa, you must be tired, or you haven't operated outside the states. How would Rex have found one?"

Marissa felt her jaw drop as she realized he was right. Rex would have looked for a forger using his tradecraft. They just needed to do the same thing and work their way through the network. Forgers knew of each other. Hell, here in India they might even have a guild of their own.

Without answering, she keyed in security passwords, brought up Tor on her laptop, and began to cruise the deep web.

Chapter Five

Comfortably ensconced in first-class, Rex felt bad for Digger in his cage in cargo, but it didn't stop him from enjoying the perks. With a mimosa in hand, he reflected on the information his research had turned up.

Changing one's looks with cosmetic surgery may sound easy, but there were numerous considerations before actually doing it. The first was how drastic a change would he want to make, and whether he'd want it to be permanent. He could assume that surgery would be permanent unless he wanted to undergo a second surgery to reverse the first, but would that even be possible?

He gave a passing thought to Catia, the stunning Mossad agent he'd met in Italy on two missions for CRC. He hadn't had time for flirtations when he worked with her on those occasions. Now that he was not in CRC's employ anymore and could determine his own comings and goings, he had time to think about her. In fact, he did so a lot, and he thought he might want to revisit that relationship. After all, there was certainly some serious chemistry between them on those occasions. She'd stirred feelings in him that no other woman had since his long-ago girlfriend, whom he'd alienated by withdrawing during the worst of his grief for his murdered parents.

Someday, maybe even someday soon, I might want her to recognize me.

He'd eventually decided he'd just have to make an appointment or two and get some opinions, because the questions he wanted to ask weren't addressed in the websites he found. All he'd discovered was that Thailand was indeed a mecca for medical tourism, renowned particularly for cosmetic surgery.

Thailand was also a popular tourist destination, especially for people from Asia, Australia, and New Zealand, as well as a popular retirement destination for people all over the world because of its high standard of living and low living costs. A peaceful country, known as 'The Land of Smiles' because of its friendly people, though his research indicated that there seemed to be a corruption problem with the government. But in Rex's opinion, across the globe, the concepts corruption and government seemed to be inseparable—the only difference between countries was that in some it just received more media attention than in others.

Rex's research showed that Thailand had a total land area of approximately half a million square kilometres. The Thai kingdom was established in the mid-14th century and was known as Siam until 1939. Thailand was the only Southeast Asian country never to be ruled by a European power. During World War II it was in alliance with Japan but became a US treaty ally in 1954 after sending troops to Korea and later fighting alongside the United States in Vietnam.

Besides the Thai language, he had some interest in their form of kickboxing, known as Muay Thai. He found it curious that such a brutal sport could have originated with such a peaceful people and looked forward to finding out the history of it as well as maybe learning some techniques for his own close-combat skills.

He was satisfied there were plenty of reasons to visit Thailand, even if he decided not to have any cosmetic surgery done after all. Even Digger would probably enjoy Thailand. Rex had discovered the medical care for pets, if there was any need for it, was on a par with veterinary care in the West, and that there were even a few off-leash parks where he could play.

The only trouble he could foresee might be in getting Digger around with him on public transportation and finding a place to stay. It seemed there were plenty of 'pet-friendly' hotels, but that might not mean friendly to pets Digger's size. But he'd cross that bridge when he came to it. His research had shown that, as in most countries in the region, a little monetary incentive offered at the right time to the right person went a long way.

His research also turned up some problems, not the least of which was sex trafficking. But that was a problem everywhere, even in places where Americans didn't expect it to be, like in their own cities. If he ran into such a situation, he'd do what he could, but he wasn't going to put a board around his neck saying, "Any issues with sex trafficking, I am your man." He hoped to enjoy some peace and quiet for a change and put the killing and CRC and his white armor aside until he felt ready to go to the US and pay those traitors who tried to kill him a visit.

The reason he most looked forward to was visiting several historic sites he'd identified. His destination, and the city he'd make his base while in Thailand, was Bangkok. Despite being a modern city, with its fair share of new skyscrapers and a thriving nightlife, it was also home to grand temples, historic relics, and incredible ancient architecture. He'd begin in the Bangkok National Museum and thoroughly explore the city while taking language lessons to accelerate his acquisition of Thai.

From there, he planned to take excursions out of town to places like Udon Thani and Sukhothai, both thought to have been established in the thirteenth century. The former was a World Heritage Site, believed to be one of the oldest settlements in Southeast Asia. Thailand's extravagant and beautiful architecture were on display in those and several other cities he'd identified.

Equally interesting, though, was a much more recent site. Near Kanchanaburi, Erawan National Park was home to a seven-tiered waterfall that drew many visitors. But Rex's interest was in the bridge made famous in a movie before he was born, whose theme song his dad had often whistled. The Colonel Bogey March, a jaunty military march tune, belied the appalling history of the bridge, built by prisoners of war as part of the Thai-Burma Railway, otherwise known as the Death Railway, during World War II. Rex still remembered seeing the movie, *The Bridge on the River Kwai*, in second-run theaters when he was a young teen. He knew the events in the movie were largely fictional, but he wanted to see the bridge anyway and visit the Kanchanaburi War Cemetery.

There were many other places to visit, too, and as the plane approached Suvarnabhumi Airport, aka Bangkok Airport, he started anticipating the landing, reuniting with Digger, and beginning to cross those bridges of his own that he'd listed. But the first stop would be for some lunch.

He was also missing Digger. There hadn't been many days when they were separated for over four hours. Rex had come a long way since putting aside his discomfort with dogs to adopt Digger.

Chapter Six

Upon arriving in Bangkok, Rex had to contend with Digger's papers not being in order. After that, he and Digger were both ravenous. After satisfying his and Digger's hunger, then giving Digger a nice long run in an off-leash park to make up for the hours in his crate in the plane, Rex's next task was to find suitable lodgings. He let his fingers do the walking, calling agents and property managers to see if they had any apartments where he could live with Digger.

After he'd amassed a list of potentials, he intended to go and look them over, Digger in tow so the managers could see him and say right away whether he'd be permitted. It's one thing to say 'my dog weighs sixty-five pounds' and another to see the big, black, shaggy reality. But traveling around the city proved to be its own challenge, as he couldn't use public transportation and several taxi and tuk-tuk operators flatly refused to take Digger aboard.

Even when he found one who was willing, he suspected the fare was heavily inflated, which he confirmed with the first agent he spoke with. That agent also looked askance at Digger and refused to show the apartment, saying Digger was far too large a dog for what their pet policy intended.

Rex was beginning to wish he'd driven to Thailand instead of flying by the time he finally found someone, an American expat, who welcomed Digger and commiserated about the transportation system. It was then that Rex began thinking about buying a tuk-tuk. He went about it with his usual thoroughness, eventually settling for a used one because it was the easiest way to cut through the red tape. He licensed it for personal use only, which meant he'd probably be stopped and questioned if he ever had a passenger. But that was a minor inconvenience, and he didn't anticipate it coming up at all.

In the latter assumption, he didn't count on what happened after he enrolled in a language school for a crash course in the Thai language. He'd learned in his research on Thailand that the Mandarin form of Chinese bore certain similarities to Thai, and in fact they shared a common origin. Having already mastered a tonal language would give him a good head start, but he wanted to learn the subtleties of the different tones and the vocabulary as quickly as possible. The influence of Old Khmer on the proto language had added vocabulary completely unfamiliar to Rex.

Three weeks of immersion in a language school environment would no doubt be faster than three weeks of misunderstandings and acquiring vocabulary by pointing and asking a passerby to name the object. It was one thing to have the knack of picking up a language without accent by immersion, and a very handy thing at that. But tonal languages were a different matter, especially related ones.

He didn't want to make the mistake of missing a tonal subtlety and saying something offensive by accident.

On the morning he went to enroll and pay for the course, his eye was caught by a distractingly beautiful woman. He was so distracted, in fact, that the bursar had to call him back to attention twice before he heard. His head had snapped all the way to the left as he caught her movement, and then swiftly snapped right as she passed behind him, his eyes following her graceful progress down the hallway until she disappeared through a side door at the end.

Wow. I knew Thailand had some beautiful women, but that one… Just, wow!

He'd arrived only a couple of days past the opening day of the course he wanted to take, and with a little palm-greasing, he successfully negotiated starting late, assuring the bursar and the academic head of the school that he wouldn't slow the rest of the class down. The next morning, he presented himself at the assigned classroom and was startled and delighted to see that same stunning woman of the previous day was his teacher.

What a stroke of luck!

Despite the distraction caused by his teacher's beauty, Rex immediately applied himself to catching up with the rest of the class. So, the first thing he learned was his teacher's name—Sunstra Chevapravatgumrong.

The question is, is that Miss Chevapravatgumrong, or Missus? If it is Miss, then the next question is if she has any… hang on, slow down, not so fast. One step at a time, Rex Dalton.

The class met daily over three weeks, for four hours a day. It didn't take him long to learn that his beautiful teacher was single, and that she spoke English quite well as far as he could find out. However, the question if she had a love interest he couldn't get answered without asking directly, and that would've been rude. He wished he could ask Digger to read her mind, because he was sure Digger read his mind—the only problem was the dog didn't comment about what he read. Encouraging though her English language skills and relationship status were, Rex decided that they'd speak Thai as much as possible when they went out. There was just one slight problem with that plan, and that he learned on the first day—the school discouraged fraternization. It was disappointing, but not insurmountable. He'd find a way. He'd already negotiated having Digger in class with him, playing the service dog card. Digger also served as an excellent wing-man, as Rex had learned before. The fact that his fellow students loved Digger was not nearly as satisfying as Sunstra's flapping about him. Of course, it went without saying, Digger was on cloud nine with all the attention.

Rex's fellow students were Asian, European, and American. Some were older, planning to retire here for the low cost of living. Others were young, of an age group known as Millennials, those born between 1981 and 1996. Although he was technically a Millennial, he was one of the oldest of the cohort, and related more to the previous designation, Generation X, those born between 1965 and 1980. Maybe it was because he was the oldest child of his parents and more had been expected of him. He hadn't been handed everything on a silver platter. He'd been expected to work for his achievements, and he had.

Many of those younger students were traveling the world, subsisting or making their fortunes as digital nomads, another slang phrase that had cropped up on Rex's radar lately. He was intrigued by the concept. Wealth had never been his motivation, but he appreciated having it now.

However, these students seemed happy, making a living off internet businesses from their laptops thus freeing themselves from the burdens that a nine to five job, working for a boss, daily commute, and the need for a permanent residence placed on people. In a way, he was doing the same— the only difference was his source of income. And very much like the Millennials, who didn't worry too much about the future, he also didn't worry about how he'd support himself once he became too old to run around and take money off bad guys. For now he was still young enough, and it wasn't as if the world would run out of bad guys soon.

Before he found a way to sidestep the school policy, and before he'd found his used tuk-tuk, Rex decided to try out some of the wildly popular pleasures on offer in Thailand, activities he'd never had the opportunity to enjoy elsewhere. In Europe, he'd been too busy, and in Afghanistan, they just didn't exist. In India there was just not enough time for it as he had to make all the arrangements to set up his new life and then found himself in a rescue operation requiring him to go to Saudi Arabia. Shortly after that he had the close encounter with CRC agents, which forced him to leave the country in a hurry. But in Thailand, he had none of those pressures, and he couldn't go anywhere without seeing ads for inexpensive massages and glittering bars in the evenings.

Rex had never had a massage other than from a physiotherapist for injuries, but never the relaxing, non-medical kind on offer here. He'd always associated the idea of it with something vaguely illicit, but on listening to the accounts some of his fellow students gave about it, it didn't sound illegal at all and definitely like one of the must-do things when visiting Thailand. He decided nothing ventured nothing gained, and if it was as good as they said, it wouldn't be a bad idea to get some of the kinks out of his muscles and joints that he'd developed over the years. He asked a few questions, got the name of a reputable place, and treated himself to one that very afternoon.

For the next half hour, as the masseuse worked on tense muscles in his back and shoulders, he relaxed more deeply than he had since he was a kid, he thought. When she got to his feet, he was sure he'd entered nirvana.

On the floor, Digger, who'd been welcomed into the spa, watched the proceedings with interest. Rex caught sight of him watching the masseuse, then checking Rex's demeanor, as if trying to understand this strange, new activity that his alpha seemed to be enjoying. It must have been puzzling to him, because the dog had never seen anyone put their hands on Rex like that without an ensuing fight.

When the masseuse indicated the massage was finished, she used simple words and gestures to indicate she'd be happy to work on the dog as well. Rex was intrigued.

What a great idea! My buddy has had as much stress as me, especially cooped up in that cage on the flight. He certainly deserves a bit of relaxation, too.

He nodded and commanded Digger to jump up on the table, which the dog did with ease. "Lie down," he said, and Digger complied.

When the masseuse started smoothing the shaggy, black fur, rubbing Digger's ears, and murmuring to him, Digger's mouth relaxed into a happy smile, and Rex thought it was going to be perfect—as nice for Digger as it had been for him. Digger even rolled on his back to let her scratch his belly.

However, soon she began to apply firmer pressure, and she must have hit a bunched nerve locus, because Digger instantly tensed, rolled, and got his feet under him as if to spring off the table. He yelped, looking at the masseuse with distrust. When she reached for him again, he snarled and snapped at her hand without making contact and gave a sharp bark.

She and Rex both interpreted it as a firm, "No!"

The masseuse backed away, even as Rex reprimanded Digger, and refused to step forward again. In rapid Thai and hand gestures, she made it clear that she was done massaging the dog.

Digger dropped off the table without being told, gave Rex a reproachful look, and nudged the masseuse's hand. He pushed his head up so her limp hand would slide down like she was petting him. Rex assumed that was Digger's way of saying, "Sorry, didn't mean to be rude. Petting is okay. Massage isn't."

He apologized to the young woman, who now had a thoroughly confused expression on her face. His Thai was not adequate to explain what his interpretation of that last interaction meant.

Contrary to Digger, Rex enjoyed the experience so much that he immediately booked three more sessions, one for every second day from that one. The first cost only ten dollars, which he thought was very cheap, but the establishment was so happy with him booking more sessions in advance, they gave him a discount of three dollars for each of the next sessions. They even told him that if he could convince Digger of the health benefits, and to not be such an ass about it, they'd give him a ten-minute massage on the house.

Rex told them he'd have a quiet word with Digger about

it but that he was not very hopeful he'd change the dog's attitude—he had a mind of his own.

———————

Since school took up most mornings, in the afternoons he visited a few places where they taught Muay Thai and observed before deciding on a school where he would take a few individual classes.

He'd settled into this routine in only a few days, so his days were full, but in the bustling city, it seemed his nights were empty even though he'd never indulged in night life outside his missions. Rex wasn't much of a drinker. He enjoyed a cocktail and especially a cold beer on a sweltering day, but going somewhere loud and crowded just to get a drink wasn't his style. Neither was going somewhere for the express purpose of meeting women. He'd already spotted the woman he thought he'd like to know better, anyway.

Nevertheless, on the Thursday after he enrolled in language school, he decided to go out and see what entertainment the city had to offer.

To his delight, Rex found a bar that allowed Digger to go in with him, where expats from all over the world congregated, and he fell into conversation with three French tourists. With the opportunity to converse in French that he hadn't enjoyed in a while, he chatted with them for several hours.

Part of Rex's uncanny facility with languages was the ability to speak any language he learned with no accent—or rather, with no accent that betrayed it wasn't his native language. Within most languages, there were regional accents, and Rex always picked up that of his learning environment. Whether he learned from a teacher, as he was doing with Thai, or from immersion in the language in a particular region of the country, he spoke with the authenticity of a native.

His new friends wanted to know what city in the south of France he'd come from. This was an unexpected wrinkle, but he hesitated only a moment before telling them he'd learned French from his father but had been raised in Italy. Surprised, they congratulated him on his fluency and accent, and then dropped the subject.

They had some spicy Thai food washed down with a few rounds of beer, and before he knew it, the time had grown quite late. Rex excused himself, saying he had school in the morning, which resulted in some merriment among the tourists. Nevertheless, he extricated himself from the situation with a smile, and left with Digger on his leash next to him.

The bar was less than a kilometer from his apartment. Rex hadn't had enough beer to impair him much, so he wasn't at first worried when he spotted three men coming toward him from the other end of the alley leading to his apartment. Although his Thai language skills consisted of only a few words, when the trio got closer, their body language didn't need any translation—they were spoiling for a fight, probably because they paid Digger no attention and saw Rex as an easy target for mugging. The reward would be some fool *farang's* bountiful wallet.

They were about eight to ten meters away when they spread out and filled the way. Rex and Digger would be forced to move up against the wall to let them pass. But he doubted that was how it was going to play out—they had their eyes fixed on him, and smug grins were playing on their faces.

Rex knew trouble when he saw it.

By the time they'd reached him, Rex and Digger had moved with their backs to the wall, and he'd decided it was best to try to defuse the situation, give up his cash without protest, and hopefully get by without a fight. It was a sketchy plan, because as he knew, muggers everywhere were bullies, and like bullies, these were probably the same as bullies everywhere. It wasn't just the money they wanted, it was likely the fight, a chance to injure someone and then brag about it to their friends afterward.

At first, true to his nature, he was tempted to teach them a few manners. He'd quickly assessed them and found them wanting, so he could kick their butts without breaking a sweat. But he soon calmed himself. He hadn't been here long. Who would the police believe? A tourist, or three locals who could claim he beat them up for no reason? And if Digger were to get in on the action, which Rex had no doubt he would, things might not work out well for the two of them. The difference in numbers alone would make cops in America believe the lone guy, even if they wondered how one guy could subdue three. But remembering the articles he'd read about corruption made him hesitate—it probably extended to the police as well.

One of them snarled at him in Thai. With his limited Thai, he tried to explain he didn't understand, while pulling out his wallet and opening it to show them he was getting out all the money he had. After his evening out, he only had about $20 in baht, which he removed and held out to them as a peace offering.

Unfortunately, Digger didn't like the idea of keeping the peace, The Land of Smiles or not, to him this undoubtedly looked like a threat to his alpha. The dog growled menacingly, his hackles up. One of the muggers said something, which Rex thought could only be a swearword. The thug aimed a kick at him, but missed when Digger anticipated it and deftly moved out of the way, then attacked his attacker. Rex realized quickly that all hell was about to break loose—defusing it was no longer an option.

The other two went for Rex, yelling in Thai, maybe more swearwords. He didn't need to know what they were saying to realize his plan was a bust and plan B was in play —neutralize the attackers as quickly as possible.

Rex stepped to the side and clotheslined the first one to reach him with a stiff left forearm. The other one was half a step behind and met Rex's vicious right hook, full in his face. Digger had taken the wind out of his man's sails with a bite to his leg, tearing his pants leg and a good bit of calf muscle with it. That guy somehow managed to shake Digger loose and was now limping down the alley in the opposite direction as fast as he could go.

Digger jumped on Rex's first attacker before he could regain his feet and stood with his forelegs on the man's chest and his muzzle practically in his face, growling. The man had both arms crossed in front of his face and was pleading for help when his buddy landed next to him, out cold and bleeding profusely from his nose, which wasn't sitting in quite the same position on his face as it had a moment before.

Rex called Digger off and let his guy get up, but he hadn't learned his lesson yet. He came at Rex again, this time ending up in a headlock, with Digger's teeth firmly planted in his ass. He could thank his lucky stars he didn't have his front turned to Digger. He screamed for mercy, and Rex called Digger off again but didn't let the pressure off the man's throat.

Calmly, Rex asked, in rudimentary Thai, "Do you understand English?"

The man grunted and nodded as well as he could, since the pressure on his throat prevented him from speaking.

Rex continued in English. "When I let you go, put your hands on your head and stand still. You do anything else, the dog will rip your ass apart and then your throat. Do you understand?"

Again, a grunt sound and an abbreviated nod assured Rex that the man understood. He let go, and the mugger's hands flew to the top of his head and stayed there. His eyes were so wide Rex could see white all around his pupils.

"Now, I want you to stay here. Your ass needs medical attention, and so does your buddy's nose. Your other buddy, the wise one who ran away, probably has a part of his leg missing. So, listen carefully to me, because I'm only going to say this once."

The man nodded.

"Keep your hands on your head, close your eyes, turn around, and slowly count to two hundred, out loud so I can hear you. You can count. Right?"

The man nodded and started counting even before his hands were on his head.

"Good boy. My dog and I are going to leave now. You stay like that until you reach the count of two hundred, then go find medical help. But remember this, if I ever hear of you molesting another tourist or anyone else for that matter, I'll find you, and you'll find out how lucky you really were tonight. Do you understand that?"

This time the nod was vigorous.

Rex continued down the alley and heard the man still counting when he turned the corner to get to the entry of his apartment block. When they got inside, he told Digger he deserved a treat and stuffed Digger's favorite toy, a Kong, with some leftover roast duck from a dinner he'd had the night before. The Kong, a hard-rubber toy shaped a little like a snowman, with a hole piercing it from the bottom, sent Digger into a near frenzy of delight as he chased it, batted at it with his paw and 'killed' it, then pegged it to the floor with his front paws and started digging out the treat inside with his tongue.

While he watched Digger's amusing antics, Rex wondered if the muggers were still in the alley and if the cops and EMTs arrived—there were no sirens he could hear. He knew the thugs in all likelihood would not give up their bad ways and would continue to mug innocent and defenseless people on the streets, but he was sure they'd definitely give a man with a big black dog a wide berth.

He shrugged. Without killing them, there was no way to ensure they wouldn't do it again, and he was out of the killing business.

"Digger, I think maybe we'd better stay out of bars and dark alleys."

Digger didn't bother to answer. He was too busy chasing the Kong, which never bounced where he thought it would.

The next day, on the Friday afternoon after school, shortly after Rex had returned to his apartment, there was knock on his door just as he was trying to decide what to do for the rest of the afternoon and the evening. It was a young guy, about eighteen or nineteen by Rex's estimation, one of the occupants in the complex whom Rex had seen but not spoken to yet.

Rex had eaten some lunch, fed and walked Digger, so he had the entire afternoon ahead of him. But it looked like the kid had something on his mind, so Rex let him in and offered him a bottle of sparkling water, all he had by way of hospitality.

The kid asked if he had any beer, but Rex didn't, and even if he did, the kid, who introduced himself as Marcel Arts, didn't look old enough to drink. His name amused Rex, too. He asked about it.

"Oh, that's my stage name, but I'm going to have it legally changed," Marcel answered. With a smirk, he added that he was on a three-year sojourn around the world to become proficient in all types of martial arts, not just the kung fu and jiu jitsu he claimed as his black-belt level expertise.

"I see," Rex answered, not giving away by word or expression what he thought of this little punk's story.

"You see, I'm planning a career as an actor in action films and I'll be doing my own stunts, not like those so-called tough guys you see on screen using subs to do that for them," Marcel continued, oblivious to Rex's cynical remark. "I figure if Chuck Norris can do it, so can I, with my looks." He obviously had no sense of his own arrogance, and Rex didn't educate him. Besides, Rex couldn't have gotten a word in edgewise, as the kid rambled on about his other heroes, Steven Seagal, the Rock, Jean Claude van Damme, and others. Rex wasn't familiar with the newer names Marcel mentioned. Movies were another of the many things that he hadn't kept up with since his recruitment to CRC.

"So, did you hear about the excitement in the alley last night?" Marcel continued blabbering without giving Rex a chance to say anything.

Not that Rex would have had much to say in any event, but when he heard this question he blinked, but Marcel wasn't watching his face. He'd assumed Rex hadn't heard about the incident and proceeded to provide a blow-by-blow description of the fight, as if he'd been there. Naturally, none of it was what had happened, but that didn't stop the kid—he had a vivid imagination.

I guess to be an actor a vivid imagination is a good trait.

When Marcel wound down, Rex asked if he'd seen the fight.

"Seen it? I was there, man! I was coming home from Millie Lin's when I heard the noise. Some poor dumb schlub was getting the shit kicked out of him, so I waded in and sent one of the perps packing. Knocked out the other two with a roundhouse kick to one's head and a sweet kung fu cross-punch I invented myself to the face of the other. The cops came and thanked me. I'm supposed to be getting a commendation soon, they said."

By that time, Rex could hardly keep a straight face, but he controlled himself and said, "Wow, that poor soul was lucky you came along."

"I'll say. That tourist could have been in real trouble if it wasn't for me." Marcel leaned forward and looked around furtively as if to make sure no one would hear what he had to say next. "Just so you know, I can hear what happens in the alley from my apartment, so if you're ever in trouble out there, just holler and I'll come and rescue you."

"Thank you very much," Rex said, barely suppressing the guffaw that rose as he tried to speak. "I'll definitely remember that."

"No problem, man. Us youngsters, we know you old guys don't think much of us, but let me tell you, my old man would skin me alive if he thought I didn't take care of people who can't take care of yourselves. I mean, they've got money and all, but they raised me right. In fact, they're the ones who sent me on this trip, isn't that cool? They support my dream of being an action superstar."

Rex had regained control of his demeanor. He answered solemnly, "It is cool indeed. You're lucky to have them."

And I'll bet they'd have paid twice as much to just get you out of their sight.

His face didn't betray the thought, though. The kid would learn his lesson soon enough, and the embarrassment would be enough punishment. Or, he wouldn't, and who knew, Rex might be reading the name Marcel Arts on a movie trailer someday.

He'd be sure to avoid seeing the film, though.

"Well, I've got to get going. I've got a date with a hot lady. I just wanted to drop by and introduce myself and offer my services. You know—never fear when Marcel is near."

"Thanks man, much appreciated. It's always good to have someone around that could help when one is in need," Rex replied while struggling to subdue a bout of raucous laughter.

"Remember my offer." Marcel winked as he got up and headed for the door.

Rex didn't want to know what kind of a date it was. He just hoped the kid was lucky enough not to contract a disease on top of his hyper-inflated ego.

When the front door closed behind Marcel, Rex turned around to see where Digger was and was surprised to see him fast asleep on the floor in the tiny living room of the apartment. It was the first time since he had met Digger that the dog completely ignored a person. He didn't even give the would-be action hero a smile, a snarl or a tail wag.

Chapter Seven

Josh and Marissa had barely agreed on a new direction for investigation in India when John Brandt called them off. He urgently wanted to find Rex, but he agreed with them that their hunt wasn't likely to yield results anytime soon. In the five or six weeks since the explosion in which he'd been presumably killed, they hadn't been able to at least confirm that Rex was either dead or alive. And something very urgent had come up, which required them to get back to the US on the first flight.

Back in the US, Brandt met them in DC and explained; in the wake of Bruce Carson's abrupt disappearance, every national three-letter alphabet agency with an investigative mission had been searching for him, with no success. Recently, a few incidents had raised the concern that he was peddling his information about past and ongoing overseas operations, and the CIA had enlisted every resource they had to find and stop him—with extreme prejudice. But so far, no one could find him.

Brandt had watched Carson board a plane for the

Marshall Islands, and he'd told everyone who would listen that's where Carson had really gone, without revealing his hand in the matter. Brandt had been kicking himself every time he thought that he'd run Carson out of town on a rail, so to speak, rather than just terminating him.

But now, the CIA had come to him, desperate for his help, asking for his best team.

In Rex's absence, for this type of operation, that was Josh and Marissa.

So, he temporarily gave up the hunt for Rex. If he knew Rex like he thought he did, and he was alive, someday, somewhere, something would turn up in the news or in rumor among the world security agencies, that would point to Rex Dalton. Brandt would be waiting and watching for it.

Meanwhile, besides himself, only three other people knew the circumstances of Carson's disappearance. One was Carson himself. The other was Marissa Bisset and now Josh Farley.

Their brief was short and to the point. Find Carson, bring him back alive, if you can. If you can't get him alive, terminate him.

Josh and Marissa understood the mission, loud and clear. They had no further questions about it. But they were puzzled about Brandt dropping the search for Rex.

"Have you heard something you aren't sharing with us, John?" Marissa asked.

"No. Nothing at all. It's just that Carson's whereabouts have become more urgent," he answered.

Something in his eyes touched Marissa's compassion, something she'd had to stuff into a separate compartment of her heart to do the work she did. "Will you have us take up the search for Rex again, after we've found Carson?"

"I'm not sure that would be productive, not the way

we've gone about it so far. Let me answer that if or when the time comes."

"Okay. You know, I like some closure to my missions," she remarked.

"And *you* know, you can't always get what you want," he said, smiling.

Marissa couldn't help finishing the quote. "But if you try sometimes, you just might find—you get what you need."

She and Josh left Brandt's office with Josh humming the Rolling Stones' song under his breath. What the United States needed now was Carson's head, on a platter or on his shoulders was up to him. After that, they'd see about getting Brandt what *he* needed.

Chapter Eight

At school, Rex turned on all his charm and, without breaking any school rules, let his lovely teacher know that he had a special interest in her. He was a little older, a world traveler, and a fascinating example of a language prodigy, which was a special interest of hers. It didn't take him long to convince her that a guided tour of Bangkok would do wonders to accelerate his grasp of the Thai language—language learning by immersion he called it.

Sunstra gave him one of her heart-stopping smiles, clearly seeing right through his whole scheme, and nevertheless, agreed.

After the first outing, he'd broken the ice enough to get her agreement to do it again. Then he asked if she was available as a private tutor, once his course ended, as he wanted to advance his fluency enough to talk with elderly people who might be able to remember history first-hand, once he started doing out-of-town excursions. As an incentive, and to let her know he had no ulterior motives, he suggested they tour historic sites in and near Bangkok as they conducted his tutoring sessions.

Sunstra told him she'd check with the school. He hadn't intended for her to do that, but he conceded she should. Happily, the school had no objection to that. They liked Rex, as he'd recommended them to several new acquaintances in the time he'd been there.

On the first of their excursions, they visited the Bangkok National Museum, one of the largest museums in Southeast Asia. Though it wasn't Rex's most fruitful way to study history, it did have the advantage of giving him an overview of the area's history as well as plenty of conversation with the beautiful Sunstra. That was his main objective, anyway. There'd be plenty of time to truly study Thailand's history when he'd finished school.

And he hoped, plenty of time to explore a deeper friendship with Sunstra when he was no longer her student.

The three weeks passed quickly, Rex was surprised to find. He'd thought at first he wouldn't be able to wait for a more intimate relationship, but the enforced restrictions on his time with Sunstra meant they were able to become deeper friends than they would have, if he'd been able to press his romantic interest. She bent the rules enough to accompany him to all the sites of historic interest in the city, and they talked the entire time about his interest in world history and languages. He told her more about himself than he'd ever told anyone, but he remained careful about the details.

He'd concocted a story when he knew he wanted to get to know her better. Like all good lies, it held an element of truth. He was a university lecturer on sabbatical, researching for a book. That was the lie. He was intensely interested in how the history of different regions interacted, how they were different, and how they were the same. That was the truth.

He might have felt bad about lying to her if he hadn't rationalized why he'd done it. It was to keep her safe from the people who would do her harm if she knew who he was.

There was however, another matter, one which was befuddling—Digger's objections to Rex and Sunstra touching each other.

What does Digger know that I don't?

Since being mauled by that vicious dog when he was a child, dog psychology was not something he was ever interested in, except of course to stay away from them as far as possible. But since circumstances forced him and Digger together he had to learn about dogs, or at least about Digger. Not that he bemoaned the fact that they were together now—they'd become best friends—but the reality was he still didn't know much about dogs. His knowledge extended only as far as Digger, what the dog taught him, and what he'd read online since they teamed up. And Digger was different, anyway. Even he could tell Digger was special—more intelligent than most dogs, not just better trained. Digger could act independently when he needed to, and whenever he did, like the time he'd followed, after Rex had been busted in Saudi Arabia for eating during the daytime during Ramadan, it was exactly the right thing to do. In human terms Digger could be described a genius.

So, Rex couldn't understand Digger's blatant animosity whenever he and Sunstra touched each other. At all other times he was happy with Sunstra. He liked it when she petted and talked to him, but the moment Rex and Sunstra got close he'd put his long black snout between them and block them from touching each other.

Do dogs get jealous?

What he could find online indicated they definitely could and did. But Digger hadn't acted jealous of the women he'd rescued from Saudi Arabia. Admittedly, Rex didn't get touchy-feely with any of those women the way he did with Sunstra.

Then it struck him.

Could that be the reason? Is it even possible, or have I lost my mind? Digger doesn't approve of a physical relationship between Sunstra and me?

I have to ask a dog's permission to date a girl!

What has the world come to? Literally gone to the dogs, it seems.

When at last the three weeks of school were past, he was free to hire Sunstra as his private tutor during the afternoons after her classes. They were also free to work on a closer relationship—something which at that stage seemed to be what they both wanted, as far as Rex could interpret Sunstra's behavior when they were together. Rex celebrated by inviting her to a fine, old restaurant in the center of the city. Anticipating that the evening might end with him and Sunstra getting closer than Digger would like, Rex left Digger at the apartment telling him, "Buddy, it breaks my heart to leave you here, but unfortunately this establishment does not allow dogs, not even ones as clever and good-looking as you."

The meal was spectacular. Rex urged Sunstra to order any delicacy she wanted and asked her to choose for him. He loved Chinese food, always had, and many Thai dishes had their origins in that cuisine. Others, though, were pure native Thai, some spicy, some creamy with rich coconut milk. He preferred the former.

He felt a little guilty for leaving Digger in the apartment. It would be too bad if it would aggravate Digger's resentment and he took it out on them the next time he was present when Rex and Sunstra were together.

It wouldn't surprise me to learn he knows I'm with her right now, even though I didn't tell him where I was going and with whom. And if he doesn't now, he will when he smells her scent on me after I kiss her goodnight.

But he couldn't ruin his evening by thinking or worrying about that. After all, he deserved to be his own man, with or without Digger's approval.

Dammit, why shouldn't I choose my own girlfriend?

Rex was surprised to see Sunstra eating with a fork and spoon, though she wielded them differently than an American would. He hadn't shared a meal with a Thai person before or noticed how they ate. Holding her spoon in her right hand, Sunstra would guide food into it with the fork, and then bring the spoon to her mouth. He was equally bemused to see his soup delivered with a Chinese spoon—something that resembled a smaller version of the cooking utensil rest his mother had kept on her stove—and a pair of chopsticks.

Where's my fork, and what am I supposed to do with these chopsticks?

Sunstra must have noticed his confusion, because she encouraged him to scoop the solid bits from his soup into the spoon with the chopsticks, then tilt the spoon to take up some broth with it. After that, Rex decided this was a clever way of doing it, and from now on he'd always eat soup that way if it had chunks of meat or vegetables, or especially noodles. It was much more efficient than chasing things around with just a spoon.

After a very sweet dessert made with sticky rice and coconut cream syrup, Rex's least favorite of the Thai dishes he'd sampled, they lingered for a while talking, and then Rex noticed Sunstra becoming restless.

"Do you need to get home soon?" he asked.

"Yes. I must be up early for school tomorrow. It has been a lovely evening, and I'd like to do it again, soon."

Rex agreed, and he was reluctant for it to end, but her signal had been clear. It was time to take her home. Maybe another evening would end differently, after they knew each other better.

They were walking down the street to where he'd parked his tuk-tuk when a few steps ahead, four men came out of a dark alley and spread out across the sidewalk. Rex's attention had been on the pavement, as he'd learned the sidewalks of Bangkok were rife with 'booby traps'. He'd steered Sunstra around an almost-invisible guide wire that would have garrotted them, warned her about an electrical cable stretched across the path, and ducked sharply when she warned him he was about to walk into a tangle of low-hanging cables.

So, her gasp of surprise and dismay took him by surprise.

It took him half a second to understand the situation, though, and prepare for the inevitable.

Sunstra was moaning, "No, no, no." She had no reason to believe he could protect her against four men, but he wasn't about to let her suffer for his inattention, although that wouldn't have made any difference to what was bound to happen next.

His eyes shifted from one to another of the thugs,

assessing their relative strengths and weaknesses while he once again tried the tactic that didn't work before to defuse the situation by offering the money in his wallet. It was clear these men had something else on their minds, though.

None of them looked at him. They each had predatory eyes on Sunstra.

One of them said something that caused her to blush in anger. Rex hadn't heard the words before, but their meaning was plain. He stepped forward to address the situation, and as soon as he moved, another one darted to the side and grabbed Sunstra by the arm.

Rex changed direction in a split second and struck with his protruding middle finger knuckle at a point just below the elbow of the thug who was grabbing Sunstra. The perp howled and involuntarily released Sunstra, grabbing at his forearm where the muscle was spasming painfully. Rex swept Sunstra behind him with his left arm and faced the guy who'd insulted her before.

It had happened so fast that two of the thugs hadn't made a move toward the fight yet. The mouthy one had a switchblade in his hand as Rex turned back toward him. Rex hated it when people pulled knives in a fist fight. It didn't scare him, but without exception it always put him in a bad mood immediately. He kicked the knife out of the guy's hand, breaking the thug's wrist in the process. The thug dropped to his knees, howling in pain.

Rex was moving to the remaining men when, from the corner of his eye, he saw a black blur take down one of the two remaining men in front of him.

Digger!

There was no time to think about it. The last man standing took a swing at Rex. He ducked below the swinging arm, punched the man in his short rib which doubled him over. Rex moved in, grabbed the thug's arm and twisted it behind his back and kicked his legs out from under him making him fall flat on his face on the pavement. Rex followed it up with a skillfully-administered kick to the head, putting that adversary out of commission for at least half an hour. The guy would have a headache for a few days, but no permanent damage that any other concussion wouldn't do.

The clock stopped just shy of four seconds—a little less than one second per hoodlum.

Rex whirled to see if it really was Digger who'd come to his aid with the fourth man. He was shocked to see his four-legged friend sitting on the prone thug, a scrap of the man's pants in his mouth, and the thug with a bloody wound on his ass, crying and calling out for help.

"Digger! How did you get out? How did you know we needed help? How did you even know where we *were*?"

With each question, Rex's voice became more emphatic and at the same time he became more confused.

Digger didn't answer, of course. He just let his smile overtake his furry face, dropping the scrap of material.

It was a mystery Rex knew he'd never solve. The only thing he could think of was that the dog hadn't taken being confined to the apartment well and had jumped out an open window to follow him to Sunstra's, then to the restaurant. Where he'd spent the hours since then, Rex couldn't imagine.

He could only be grateful for the help. Taking down that fourth guy might have made him a little out of breath.

However, when he glanced at Sunstra, the distress on her face worried him. Was she upset about the men attacking, or because he'd been a bit too rough with the thugs, or worse, had he shown too much of his fighting skills?

Sunstra tried to keep what was flashing through her mind from her expression as she looked at Ruan warily. Her brother, who was in the Thai navy, had seen to it that she could defend herself before she'd moved to the city. But against four men, she'd have had no chance.

But who was this *farang* whose company she'd come to enjoy? Who could defeat three healthy, fighting fit, and rough men before she could blink her eyes twice? From what she'd observed, he'd have had no trouble with the fourth, either, if the dog hadn't come to his aid.

She'd seen a lot of Muay Thai fighting in her lifetime, but she'd never seen anything like what this man had just done. She had to shake her head a few times, as if to rewind the video to remind her what she saw. It looked more like a blur to her than one man moving around taking three mean guys out in a few seconds. One move she was actually certain she'd seen, not imagined, the kick that disarmed the one with the knife, looked like a Muay Thai action.

Where did Ruan learn that? For that matter, where did he learn any of this stuff? Who is this man?

And Digger.

How is it possible that this soft-spoken, well-mannered man and his friendly service dog could become so viciously violent one moment and the next moment behaved as if nothing'd happened?

She hadn't had much experience with support animals. Most of what she'd encountered before had been seeing-eye dogs. This dog seemed to have superhuman—or super-dog—capabilities.

Service dog? Not likely. More like fighting partner.

There's more here than Ruan has led me to believe.

University lecturer? Not likely, either.

Despite her misgivings, the adrenaline from the scare suddenly left her, causing her to start shaking and her knees to buckle. Ruan was there in a heartbeat, supporting her and smoothing her hair.

"Hey, it's all right, Beautiful Eyes. These guys won't be attacking anyone else anytime soon. Let's get out of here," he said.

As soon as the man took her in his arms, the dog was there between them, pushing them apart.

"What did I do to make you hate me?" she asked, staring at Digger.

The dog responded with a soft, non-threatening growl, which earned a rebuke from Ruan. She didn't want that—they were obviously a team, and from what she'd seen, that's how it was meant to be.

But, who is this man and his dog? He's not a criminal, he's not a university lecturer, he doesn't look and act like a soldier or a policeman. What is he hiding?

She was silent as they rode in the tuk-tuk to her apartment, Digger in the back seat as he'd always been when she was with Ruan. She mulled over the times Digger had seemed unfriendly, though other times he'd been fine, like when she scratched behind his ears. It occurred to her then that Digger didn't hate her. He just didn't want her to get too friendly with Ruan.

But why? That's strange behavior for a dog, well, as far as her knowledge of dogs went. She looked at him and thought, *So, you're just jealous then. Is that it?*

Digger didn't look at her. He had his head stuck out of the tuk-tuk and his tongue hanging out.

Well, Digger, I've got news for you. You just have to get over it, because as of tonight, this man, Ruan or whatever his real name is, is important to me.

It wasn't just his heroics with the attackers that attracted her to him. It was the gentle way he treated her, the way he respected her, the way he looked at her. It was the fun they'd had at dinner, and on other occasions, his dry humor and wittiness at times, his willingness to try new experiences, his honesty when he didn't like them. She suppressed a giggle at the memory of the face he'd made when he tasted the *Khao Neow Toorien.* She'd been so sure he would like it, but it seemed he didn't appreciate how sweet it was.

If only I could know who he really is.

Ruan told Digger to stay in the tuk-tuk when he walked her to her door. She understood why he told Digger to stay behind when he took her into his arms again and pressed a kiss to her cheek. She'd turned her head when she saw his intent. It was too soon for him to kiss her lips. He seemed to take it in stride, but she saw the disappointment in his eyes. She was also a bit disappointed about her reaction, but she followed her emotions, which told her to take a bit of time to think about the surprising side of him she'd seen tonight.

There'll be a next time, and a next... and maybe... many more.

Rex was still unsettled about the end to the night when he and Digger got back to the apartment. The first thing he did was check the windows. Sure enough, a window in the bedroom was open about eight inches. Rex looked at Digger in disbelief.

"Did you really wiggle out through that? And if you didn't catch up with me, how did you think you would get back in?" It didn't seem possible, but he couldn't find another plausible answer. To think Digger could have done it in time to follow him in the tuk-tuk was even more of a puzzle, but the evidence was there, irrefutable.

Digger tilted his head at the question. Rex shook his head and went into the little kitchen to stuff Digger's Kong with peanut butter, a special treat. His help had been timely, and there was no point in scolding him for his escape. In any event, it seemed a little insulting to a dog as intelligent as Digger to treat him like an unruly child. Although, there was still the matter of his behavior when it came to Rex and Sunstra touching each other.

Digger was making his usual amusing fuss over the Kong when a knock at the door put Rex on full alert. He hadn't even looked to see if there were witnesses when he'd hastily led Sunstra away from the fallen thugs. Chances were, he'd open the door to an angry Thai police officer. But he had no choice. If he was in trouble for defending himself and Sunstra against superior numbers, he'd just have to get an attorney and fight the charges. At least he could count on Sunstra being an honest witness.

He opened the door with a hard look on his face, which he smoothed instantly when he saw it was only Marcel Arts, the silly kid from down the hall.

What the hell does he want at this time of night?

Oblivious to Rex's abrupt change in expression or apparently the time of night, Marcel swaggered into the room and took a seat uninvited. He ignored Digger and started to tell Rex about a confrontation he'd had with some mugger earlier.

Must be muggers' night out, Rex thought.

Rex didn't answer, and it didn't faze Marcel. He continued with a stream of verbal diarrhea giving a blow-by-blow description of the fight, without a doubt all of it imaginary, and then, without waiting for a comment, or stopping to take a breath, went straight into how tough his training was and what a lethal fighter he'd become.

"You should have seen it, man! I was poetry in motion. Just like that old guy, Muhammed Ali. 'Float like a butterfly, sting like a bee.' That asshole didn't know what hit him. Ka-pow!"

Marcel punched the air with a quick right-left. Rex still hadn't had an opening to even say 'hello' or 'please come in, have a seat'. He couldn't have without interrupting the punk, and he thought the quickest way to get it over was to just remain quiet and ride out the tsunami of bullshit coming out of the boy's mouth and let him go.

"You should come on down and train with me," Marcel said. "I'll put in a word for them not to go real hard on you until you get the hang of it. I mean, you're not flabby, like some old dudes. You could get in shape, if you tried. Everyone ought to know a little self-defense. I mean, I won't always be around to get you out of a scrape, right?"

"Hmm, I don't know about that. I'm not a violent man —I'm a pacifist. I abhor any form of violence," Rex said, when Marcel finally paused for an answer.

"Oh, yeah, sure I understand that, but some day you're going to land in a position where you'd have no choice. You'll then have to choose, you die or you fight. Just think about it, though. I mean, you don't have to try to go pro, like me. Just enough to defend yourself, right?"

"Right," Rex said. "I'll think about it." He fell silent, not wanting to encourage the kid to stay any later. Digger had finished getting all the peanut butter out of the Kong and was looking at Marcel, just staring like he didn't quite know what to make of the kid.

"Hey, nice dog you got there. What's its name?"

"*His* name is Digger," Rex answered.

Digger lifted his ears slightly and looked at Rex. Then he went back to staring at Marcel.

"Funny name. Does he dig holes in the yard? My folks had a dog that pretty much destroyed our garden with all the holes he dug. In the end my dad shot it. Can't have a dog doing that."

Rex hadn't particularly liked the kid before, but at that moment, he developed an active dislike for Marcel *and* his dad, who seemed to be someone who deserved obnoxious offspring like this kid.

"Marcel, I hate to cut this short, but I need my beauty rest," he said, working to keep the revulsion out of his voice.

"Oh, yeah, sure. My grandpa's like that, too. Always wanting to go to bed early. Not like my folks. They're party animals." He grinned, got up, and sauntered to the door. "Think about those self-defense lessons," he said. "This is a dangerous city at night."

Rex closed the door quietly behind Marcel, although he wanted to slam it, preferably with Marcel's head jammed in it.

"Digger, please promise me whenever I see that kid you'll remind me why I shouldn't knock the punk on his arrogant ass," he said.

Digger grinned for the first time since Marcel had knocked on the door.

"I'll take that as a yes."

Chapter Nine

On the Monday a week after he took Sunstra to their first dinner, Rex was ready for his first side trip. He'd seen Sunstra for dates a couple more times in the previous week, making sure that all the apartment windows were firmly closed when they were going somewhere Digger wouldn't be welcome. They worked on his language skills while cruising the city in his tuk-tuk, Digger in attendance at those times. The dog still objected any time Rex got physically close to Sunstra, but then she didn't seem especially anxious to do more than hold hands and occasionally let him kiss her cheek.

Rex had a few dalliances over the years whenever he was on compulsory R and R after missions for CRC, all of them nice and short and with no strings attached. But in reality, he didn't have any more experience with women than he did with other dogs than Digger. He'd had a steady girlfriend, long ago, but it felt like it was in another life. At the time, he'd even intended to propose to her. But then the tragedy had occurred, a terrorist attack on a Spanish railway station that killed his parents and two younger siblings. The peaceful young man who'd loved that girl and who'd looked forward to a career in the US Foreign Service was emotionally damaged in that attack, and he'd transformed into the brooding, angry man who'd joined the Marines to avenge his losses. From there he was recruited into Delta Force and trained as a Special Forces operator and from there into the black ops outfit, CRC, where he was trained as one of the world's most lethal assassins—a capacity in which he rained terror, destruction, and death on the enemies of the US.

But Rex wasn't that man anymore, either. He'd burned out the anger in rooting out terrorists, drug and arms dealers who supported and financed them, and even in killing a few people who'd needed killing but weren't part of his official assignments. His current nomadic life was his attempt to get away from all of that.

For those reasons, his attraction to Sunstra was a new experience for him.

Not wanting to make a misstep, he told himself to let her set the pace. He wasn't in a hurry to move a romance along, even though to some extent, he was allowing long-repressed urges to inform his feelings for her. Therefore, when he'd achieved enough fluency in the language to feel he could get along on his own, he picked one of the sites he'd listed for exploration and took his leave for a week of travel.

From his research about the country he'd done since arriving, he knew the relatively modern history of Udon Thani wasn't the most interesting part for someone like him. The area had been occupied since prehistoric times, as evidenced by paintings thought to be six-thousand years old on the unusual rock formations within the Phu Phra Bat historical park. More recently, the park's temples and shrines showed hints of Dvaravati and Khmer culture. Rex planned to drive there in a rented car, and then on the way back, take a side trip to Phanom Rung, another historical park.

The temple complex built between the tenth century and thirteenth at Phanom Rung was said to be stunningly preserved. Rex had another interest in it, as the temple complex was initially Hindu, but later became Buddhist. It was arranged to mirror the Hindu god Shiva's heaven.

On his return to Bangkok, he called Sunstra to resume their afternoon language lessons, and when he picked her up from her apartment that afternoon, she greeted him so enthusiastically he got the distinct impression that she'd missed him as much as he had missed her. He couldn't help but think there might be the prospect of moving their relationship to the next level.

Clearly he'd already forgotten that Digger had claimed the right, like an over-protective parent, to have a say in this relationship.

They talked, in Thai of course, about expats in Thailand that day as she took him to various street-markets and helped him shop to restock his pantry and refrigerator. The subject matter was her choice.

Later on, the conversation moved to places to visit while in Thailand, and Rex didn't detect an ulterior motive until she asked if he would consider making Pattaya his permanent home.

"What gave you the idea I was looking for a permanent home in Thailand?"

Rex had been studying her face closely, and for a fleeting moment she appeared a bit crestfallen with his answer. However, the expression quickly changed into a smile as she shrugged and said, "No, nothing you did gave me that idea, it's just that Pattaya is such an idyllic place, many people who visit it want to make it their permanent home."

It was the first time since laying eyes on her, weeks ago, that Rex got the impression that she was not entirely candid with him.

He tried to repair his faux pas. "Pattaya seems to be one of the most sublime places I'll ever have the pleasure to visit, but the thought of living there permanently hadn't crossed my mind, not yet. And even if it does when I visit it, my finances have limitations. I'll have to go back to America when my sabbatical is over."

It sounded like the truth, even to him, and then he had a sudden flash of insight.

Could it be that Sunstra asked that question because she's thinking of a more serious relationship? One where we are living in Pattaya?

He mulled the idea for a few brief seconds. *That's what you want, Dalton. Isn't it? You're the one who felt attracted to her at first sight. You made the first move and bent the rules so you could be with her. Why the sudden ambivalence?*

He became aware of her gaze on him, studying his face as he'd stopped walking and was staring into the middle distance.

Then it hit him between the eyes like a sledgehammer. *I'm not ready for it. I can't make a long-term commitment, not to her and not to any woman, for that matter. I'm the one who's unable to settle down, not yet.*

He was shaken out of his reverie by her voice, "What is it Ruan? What are you staring at?"

Rex almost sighed in relief, grateful that his face didn't betray what just went through his mind. There was no way he could reveal that to her. So, he had to spin something, "Sorry, your question just got me thinking how much I have been enjoying the freedom of my sabbatical, and in a few months it'll be over." He smiled at her and added, "This is the kind of lifestyle I can get used to."

She laughed and said, "I guess anyone can get used to it. But, let's not dwell in the future, nor in the past, let's enjoy the here and now."

Rex smiled at her, "You're very wise, Sunstra. Let's do that."

Rex took her hand, and she let him, as they started walking again in silence. A minute or so later, Rex looked around and saw Digger walking on Sunstra's side and then realized Digger didn't try to separate them as he always did.

Buddy, one day I hope I'll be able to figure out your psyche.

But Rex knew that it was his duty to cease and desist from pressing for a more physical relationship with Sunstra unless he was prepared to allow himself to love her. The problem with that was what he'd just discovered, with a shock—he was not in the emotional space to do so. Yet, he had a longing to be with her, touch her, and hold her. What was that? Hormones?

Jeez, this relationship thing is complicated.

And if the situation with Sunstra was not enough to do his head in, the image of a certain Israeli woman he'd met in Italy popped into his mind's eye. While he owed Catia nothing, least of all fidelity, he did owe Sunstra an unencumbered heart if he pursued anything more with her than platonic friendship.

"What's there in Pattaya that's of historic importance?" he asked. Rex hadn't forgotten his mission to explore the idea of changing his appearance. He'd just put it on the back burner after meeting Sunstra, intending to take it up again when he left Bangkok for good. As it happened, Pattaya offered some of the best options in cosmetic surgery, but he also needed to keep his cover—his interest in Thai history—intact for Sunstra.

"Well, it was conquered by an invading Burmese army in 1757, I think," she offered.

Rex snatched at the straw. "Then I'll certainly go and see what it has to offer," he answered. "It's only a couple of hours by car, right?"

"About that."

"I'll go next week. Meanwhile, where would you like to have dinner tonight?"

They moved past the awkwardness of the earlier conversation and went back to shopping. She'd opted to invite him to her apartment for a home-cooked Thai meal. Inwardly, Rex groaned. She was going to make it difficult for him to remain a gentleman. But who would turn down a home-cooked meal? He hadn't had anything like that in weeks, except for his own indifferent cooking skills. He remembered delicious home-cooked meals in India, with dishes he'd never have tried in restaurants. What Thai delicacies would he discover in Sunstra's cooking?

The following week, Rex invited Sunstra to go with him to Pattaya, though her presence might cramp his investigations of cosmetic surgery options. He could always go again, since it was so close. But she'd described the beaches and tourist attractions with such gusto he thought she'd like the outing. Unfortunately, she couldn't arrange a substitute teacher for her classes, so in the end she had to decline.

Rex planned to spend just one night there, along with the days on either side, and return to Bangkok on a Friday evening. He left early on Thursday, Digger at his side in the rented car's front passenger seat. The dog had begun asserting his right to the spot any time Sunstra wasn't with them, which made Rex think part of his behavior was territorialism, too. But then again, Digger had stopped separating them whenever they got close since they'd cleared the air about where their relationship was going, or rather, where it wasn't.

Despite the crowded highway and the slow-down at the toll booths, Rex made it to Pattaya while morning was still fresh. He had made appointments at two cosmetic surgery clinics and one hospital to look over his options, and he just had time for a snack and to walk Digger before attending the first one.

He wasn't impressed with the offices, or with the doctor, who seemed to want to completely reconstruct him as if he was a dilapidated car in need of an extreme makeover. As he hurried out of that office, thinking he'd barely escaped with his gender intact, he hoped the next two would offer more reasonable and considered opinions.

He liked the next doctor, a woman.

Her first reaction upon hearing his question was to ask, "Why would you want to change those looks? You are a very handsome man."

Rex almost never blushed. On the few occasions he did, his tan complexion usually hid it very well, but in this instance he was sure the woman could see it. "Uh, thank you? To answer your question, well, why does anyone want to change their looks? So as not to be recognized, right?"

She smiled and shook her head. "No. Actually, why most people want to change their looks is to correct a flaw. In other words, to look better, more attractive, to feel better about themselves. Younger people like yourself usually want to fix too-large or crooked noses, or an under-developed chin, wingnut ears, crooked teeth and stuff like that. As people mature, getting older, some want to take a few years off their looks.

"Those are the usual motivations to undergo the procedure, but in your case, I'm intrigued. Why don't you want to be recognized?"

Rex realized he hadn't thought it through. He hadn't expected such a probing questioning session.

Is medical information privileged here? If I answer honestly, does she have to keep it confidential? Nah, not going to run the risk.

But Rex was a quick thinker, and over the last few months he'd been in many tight situations where that skill was tested. He still wanted to play the doctor-patient privacy card, so, he asked her if what he was about to tell her will remain private.

She told him it was the same in Thailand as in the US and other countries, what he told her was safe with her and protected by law.

So, Rex launched into a story that he made up on the fly and that had him almost smiling about all the BS coming out of his own mouth as he told the doctor he'd been trying to get away from a vengeful, stalking ex-wife. Apparently this ex-wife had a very rich and influential 'family', he made air quotes around the word 'family' trying to create the impression he was referring to the mob, who kept on tracking him down wherever he tried to hide. He'd had enough of her and her damn 'family', and the only way he could think of getting away from them was to 'disappear' in this manner.

He was half out of breath after explaining all of that and sat back to wait for the doctor's reaction, thinking he sounded so convincing, even to himself, she would've bought it.

But she shook her head.

"That's not a very good reason, Mr. Winterbottom," she said.

Rex almost started laughing, *How the hell did I come up with an alias like Winterbottom?* But somehow he maintained his composure and kept on listening.

"You'll regret it, I'm sure. I'm in the business of fixing what's broken so to speak, and you know the old saying, don't try to fix what ain't broken.

"There isn't much I could do for you that wouldn't change your looks for the worse, and I'll not be able to live with my conscience if I'm the one who'd damaged a pretty face like yours. When I treat people, they look better and feel better about themselves afterward. In your case, you'll want to kill me every morning when you look in the mirror.

"I'm sorry, but I'm not the answer to your wife problems."

Rex didn't have a ready answer for that, so he shrugged. "Do you have any other suggestions? I mean of the non-surgical, temporary kind."

She said, "You could dye your hair, or in your case, bleach it and then dye it. Another option is to shave it all off and dye your eyebrows. Believe me, your own mother wouldn't recognize you, not to mention your ex-wife or her 'family",'" she also made air quotes around the word 'family'.

"Combine any of those with a pair of horn-rimmed glasses and you'd look distinguished as well as being totally unrecognizable.

"None of those changes are permanent and it's fairly easy to maintain for as long as you want, or until your ex-wife finds another man and leaves you alone," she concluded with a smile.

Rex thanked her for her honest opinion and left, considering what she'd said.

"Digger, I'm not sure what you think, but I think that was sound advice. Much better than cutting up such a pretty face as mine," he said and chuckled as he looked down at Digger's smiling face.

"Thanks buddy, I knew you would agree."

With that, Rex set aside the whole question of cosmetic surgery.

That night, Rex decided to take in the nightlife, though he'd had enough of doing that on his own in Bangkok. He and Sunstra had fun, though, and he had to admit he missed her. In the end, he felt it would be better to go out than sitting in a hotel room with only Digger for a companion and moping about Sunstra's absence. Digger had been quite patient with him as he made the rounds of his doctor appointments, though, so he planned to take his buddy with him, and only go into establishments that didn't mind the dog being with him.

They had dinner at a restaurant with sidewalk tables, where Digger stayed underneath. Other dogs were less discreet, begging at their owner's tables with no manners at all. Rex was grateful for Digger's good manners, not begging, patiently waiting for the tidbits Rex occasionally slipped him. It was a rare treat for Digger, and one that Rex knew he wouldn't take advantage of later.

After a few hours of having his eardrums assailed by awful bands, whose singers had no idea how bad they were when they tried to sing in English, Rex decided he was risking deafness or insanity or both if he stayed any longer. Neither appealed to him, so he and Digger left, and the eagerness with which Digger got up and out from under the table gave him the impression that the dog was relieved to be getting away from the cat stranglers.

As usual, Rex and Digger were both aware of their surroundings, taking in everyone and everything around them without looking as if they were paranoid. They were about a two minutes walk away from the restaurant with the horrible band when Rex saw and heard a commotion a couple of blocks ahead, a young girl being pulled into an alley by three men. Rex expected people who were closer than him and Digger to rush to the aid of the young girl.

Yet no one even appeared to notice. No one moved toward the alley, not even at a leisurely pace. Everyone just went on about their business, as if they couldn't hear the girl's screams or see her struggling with three full-grown men.

Damn, what's wrong with these people? They don't want to see or hear, they're just going to let that girl fend for herself. Almost like the three monkeys; I didn't see anything, I didn't hear anything, and therefore I won't say or do anything.

Rex glanced at Digger and saw he was just waiting for the command. "Let's do it," he said and broke into a sprint.

Digger was more than five yards ahead of him in less than a second.

"Get out of my way, sheeple!" Rex shouted to the people coming toward him on the sidewalk. They parted like the Red Sea before Moses' staff to keep from being bowled over by Rex and Digger. Rex kept his eyes on the alley entrance where the girl had disappeared from his view. He just hoped the men wouldn't drag the girl into a building or down another alley before he got there. But then he saw it was clear Digger understood where they were going— he'd get there long before Rex could and would show him where they went if necessary.

He was several yards away from the corner around which Digger had disappeared when a ferocious barking and snarling issued from the darkness ahead. Rex skidded around the corner and had to stop quickly not to run full-tilt into the tangle of snapping dog, dodging ruffians, and the screaming girl. He hesitated for a split second to assess the situation before wading in and slugging the guy who had hold of the girl's arms. She was so much shorter than the hood who had her. Rex's right fist landed unencumbered front and center in the thug's face. His arms around the girl flew to the sides as the full force of the blow lifted him off his feet and landed him on his ass. His hands were clutching at his broken nose.

With his left hand, Rex snatched the girl out of the tangle and thrust her toward the closest wall, while using the other arm for balance as he placed a high kick into the face of a second thug. The guy dropped, out of commission with a broken jaw, and the copious bleeding from his nose indicated it was also broken. Rex had let go of the girl, so he used both arms to flip the second thug on his face, so he wouldn't drown in his own blood.

The third man was fully engaged with Digger. He had a knife and was slashing at the dog wildly. Seeing the knife instantly brought his blood to boiling point. In that moment, Rex knew what it would feel like to be a father whose child was being threatened by a thug with a knife. He took only a moment to look toward the girl, and saw she hadn't run as he expected, before he moved in to keep Digger from being sliced by the knife-wielding asshole. He couldn't kick at the guy without potentially catching Digger with the kick, and he couldn't grab him without getting cut himself.

"Digger, down! Sound off!"

Digger dropped to his belly at the command and emitted the hair-raising howl the second command ordered. The man with the knife jerked in surprise and gave Rex the opening he needed. Rex grabbed the thug's knife arm at the wrist with his right hand and with the open palm of his left hand he hit the man's elbow from below while forcing his wrist down, it snapped like a dried twig. The knife fell to the ground followed almost simultaneously by an ear-splitting shriek of pain.

Rex kicked the knife away and saw the girl go after it before he swiped the hooligan's legs from under him which landed him flat on his back next to his mates.

"Digger, sound off."

Digger started howling and barking.

Rex didn't want to just walk away from the scene with the girl, he wanted these guys permanently out of business. He hoped that Digger's barking and howling would eventually draw the attention of the cops, though he didn't hold out much hope that any of the locals or tourists in the area would get involved. He could see the girl was a very young teen, or possibly a pre-teen. It didn't take a lot of imagination to figure out what would have happened to her if he hadn't intervened. Digger seemed to understand, though, as he ran to the end of the alley where it connected with the main street and kept on making noise.

Rex kept a wary eye on the thugs as he addressed the girl. "What are you doing out here at this time of night? Where are your parents?"

She lifted her chin. "I went to meet my boyfriend. I was just going home."

"How old are you, anyway?" Rex demanded, while thinking about what he'd say to the 'boyfriend', if he were here.

"I'll be fourteen soon."

"How soon?"

She dropped her eyes. "In ten months."

Rex couldn't believe it. "Do your parents know you went to see your boyfriend? Where is *he*?"

She didn't answer, and Rex drew his own conclusions. From the way she was dressed, she'd sneaked out of the house and met her boyfriend, or possibly an older man, for a purpose her parents would no doubt be appalled to discover. The fact that the boyfriend hadn't seen her safely home told him that it was probably not a relationship her parents would have approved of at all.

Rex couldn't decide whether he was sad for the girl or angry at her recklessness. Maybe a bit of both. He'd already made up his mind that he would insist on seeing her home, with or without the police, and informing her parents of what had happened.

Almost as if on cue, Digger came running toward him, with a couple of cops in hot pursuit. Rex mentally thanked Sunstra for his fluency in Thai as he explained why he was in an alley with an underage girl and three young men, two of them unconscious and bleeding from the nose and a third with a broken elbow.

The two policemen looked at the thugs, then at Rex, and then at each other.

Oh, oh here it comes.

It took a considerable amount of time to persuade the cops that Rex did so much damage on his own. The cops asked the girl, and she told them it was only Rex. They didn't want to believe it, neither did they want to believe that Rex came to her rescue nor had any nefarious intentions. It was only after the cops did a bit of screaming and shouting at the one with the broken arm that he told them it was Rex, and Rex only, who kicked their asses. However, he tried to explain that they did nothing wrong and that Rex assaulted them without cause.

Rex and Digger stood off to the side and watched the disagreements. He'd given his explanation, and if the cops didn't want to believe him then it was better to not say anything further. The arguments were still going on when another cop turned up on the scene, had one good look at the thugs, and told his colleagues that he knew these hooligans and that he was extremely pleased with their condition. He knew them to be trouble makers that had for months been terrorising people on the streets in Pattaya but had so far been lucky enough to escape arrest.

He also found it a bit rich that a guy of Rex's size and posture could mete out so much punishment to three street-fighters without a single scratch to himself, and with so little effort, it seemed. However, he said he didn't care who did it. As far as he was concerned, whoever did it deserved praise not hassles.

With the last cop's favoritism, the matter was quickly

settled. The cops thanked Rex and took custody of the thugs, cuffing the one who'd had the knife.

Rex decided he didn't need to tell them the girl had taken the knife. He figured if the lecture he was going to give her didn't take, she might as well have a weapon to defend herself, because she would need it.

The officers seemed torn about splitting their team so one could take the girl home while the other took the thugs to jail. Rex explained that he intended to talk to the girl's parents anyway, so he'd be glad to take her home.

The girl began to protest loudly that she could get herself home and who was he to talk to her parents about what was her business. One cop looked at the other and muttered something along the lines of 'better him than me'. The other agreed, and without another word, turned their backs on Rex and the girl.

Rex took that as his cue to leave. He took the girl by her upper arm and said, "Let's get you home."

"Let me go."

"I don't think so. I take you home and talk to your parents, or I ask the police to take you home and I accompany them, and I still talk to your parents. Which is it going to be?"

She refused to answer.

"Tell me where you live, or shall I ask the dog to get it out of you?"

It was an idle threat. He'd never have commanded Digger to attack a teen-aged girl, unless she was a terrorist. This girl was just a misguided kid, but she did take the threat seriously. Sullenly, she told him her address.

He allowed her to jerk her arm out of his hand and said, "Let's go."

He walked on one side of her and Digger walked on the

other, until they came to her parents' house a few blocks away. She said the door would be locked, as she'd gone out her window, so Rex knocked loudly.

It was past two a.m., so he wasn't surprised when an angry shout for him to go away came from inside. He knocked again, and a two-minute wait produced an angry man, who snatched the door open with a curse. It died on his lips as he spotted his daughter with the *farang*.

At 5'11", Rex wasn't a big man by Western standards, but he stood a head taller than the girl's father. The man's expression changed from anger to astonishment and back to anger in a matter of the blink of an eye. In rapid Thai, he addressed his daughter, who hung her head and started to shove past him. Rex caught most of it, though it was faster speech than he could follow. He hastened to correct the impression the father had gotten.

"Sir, your daughter was attacked by several men, who dragged her into an alley. I have brought her home to you, so she'd remain safe. But if you don't mind, I'd like to give her some advice."

"She did not sneak out of our home to sell herself to you?" the man demanded.

Evidently, he was reassured by the revulsion on Rex's face, as he opened the door wider and asked him in.

"I don't buy women, and that includes little girls," Rex couldn't help but say.

"I am sorry. This child has been a trial. She has got involved with the wrong friends, and we cannot control her."

"I can see that. Maybe tonight's experience will help persuade her that she's not old enough or tough enough to handle herself out there."

The girl stood with her arms crossed. "I'm right here. Don't talk about me like I can't hear you."

It was enough for Rex. He made his voice stern and looked her in the eyes. "Young lady, I don't know you, but I do know men. You may think the clothes you're wearing might make you look cool, the latest fashion, but all you're doing by dressing up like that is sending a message to every scumbag of a man out there that you're available. Your boyfriend may be a gentleman, or not, but you've seen tonight what happens when a young girl walks down the street in a getup like that, with no one to protect her from harm. If I were you, I'd pay more attention to what my parents tell me. Next time, there might not be anyone to help you. There were many people on the street tonight who saw what happened and none of them wanted to get involved, they all hastened to get away from the scene."

The stubborn set of her jaw let him know his words were going in one ear and out the other.

Opening the door to leave, he glanced at her father. He was staring at Rex, so Rex nodded slightly, and the father followed him outside.

"What did you mean about her boyfriend?" he asked. "What boyfriend?"

Rex told him what the girl had said about a boyfriend, and his thought that the boyfriend might be an older man, concluding that anyone who cared about her would have driven or walked her home. The father nodded.

"I will get to the bottom of this. Thank you. You have not only saved my daughter from a terrible ordeal, but you have opened my eyes. We will try to keep a better watch on her now. If that doesn't work, we'll have to move away from here, so she can get away from the influence of her friends."

"It was nothing. I hope she stays safe."

To Digger, Rex said, "Come on, boy, we need to get some sleep." And when he was sure he was out of earshot of the girl's father he said, "Digger, let me tell you, it seems to me it is a lot of trouble, and it takes a lot of effort, to raise a human."

Rex was more troubled about the incident than he had been since he'd left Afghanistan where he'd saved a boy from an abusive grandfather. The girl he'd saved tonight was likely to become a victim again, and next time he wouldn't be there. He thought about Rekha and her former harem-mates. Would she be okay without him watching her all the time? How much good was he really doing, when he was only one man and it was only by accident that he was available to handle these incidents. What would happen to Sunstra when he was gone?

He tossed and turned until nearly dawn, trying to understand his purpose in life. Was it to wander, gathering historical facts and taking pictures of ruins? Or was it to make a difference in the world by eradicating bad guys? Had he made a mistake by hiding from CRC?

He wished Sunstra were there, so he could talk to her, not so much about what was troubling him—that would have blown his cover—but she had a way of always talking about interesting things, which, tonight, would've taken his mind off the fretting.

At last, with the image of Sunstra's beautiful eyes in his mind, he drifted off to sleep. Without Rex's notice, Digger had kept vigil over his troubled friend. When Rex's breathing became regular, Digger closed his eyes, too.

Chapter Ten

Rex had intended to spend the following day exploring the historical sites in Pattaya, but his late night resulted in sleeping late that morning. When he woke, his energy and outlook on life were both down, no doubt because of the young girl he'd saved from physical harm but couldn't do much for her future.

And of course, he missed Sunstra.

"Shall we just go on back to Bangkok, boy?" he asked Digger.

Whether Digger understood the question or was just his normal, happy-go-lucky self, he widened his mouth in a dog smile and wagged his tail. Rex took it for an affirmative and called for his car to be brought around.

On the drive back, he did everything he could to keep his mind off the events of the previous night and early morning, with limited success. If that was not enough to be upsetting, he couldn't stop thinking about Sunstra. He had confused himself so much about her he didn't know what to think anymore. One moment he knew he was not ready to settle down and pursue a serious relationship with her, and the next moment he missed her and couldn't stop thinking of her. On the one hand he knew he shouldn't give her false signals unless he was ready to love her, on the other hand he thought it was too late, he was already in love with her.

But how the hell would I know anything about love? I thought I loved Jessie, but I dumped her. Now I think I love Sunstra, but I can't tell her. What's wrong with you, Rex Dalton? Seems like you should rather go and see a shrink than a cosmetic surgeon.

Rex tried, for a while, to think of it as a mission, a mission to sort out this emotional seesaw about the relationship with Sunstra. But that didn't work. There was no target to be the focus of his wrath. There was only this target with the most beautiful eyes, a knee-buckling smile, and a personality to match. Nobody to kill, only somebody to love or not.

Damn, ordinary life is stressful, if you ask me.

Between that and the traffic, he was no closer to an answer, and in a foul mood, by the time he got back. So he was in no way willing to put up with Marcel Arts, who accosted him at the entrance to the apartment building.

"Not right now, Arts," he snapped.

"Jeez, who pissed in your coffee?" the kid remarked. But, fortunately for him, he went on by without bothering Rex any further.

After getting Digger and his overnight kit into the apartment, Rex felt bad about his surliness. He promised himself he'd make it up to the kid the next time he saw him.

Rex decided that his mood would be much improved if he could see Sunstra. Since it was a Saturday, he gave her a call and suggested a picnic, and he was happy that she accepted. Apparently, their awkward conversation of a few days ago hadn't discouraged her from seeing him. He'd never, not since losing his parents, had a friend who wasn't also a comrade in arms until meeting the Gyan family and Aarav Patel in India.

It didn't keep him from understanding that sooner or later he'd have to decide what to do with his life. He was too young to spend the rest of his life on his own, with no purpose other than to visit interesting historical places and, it seemed, stumbling upon unwanted trouble. But he decided for today, he'd enjoy Sunstra's and Digger's company, put last night's events out of his mind, and avoid thinking about the future.

The picnic in the park and Digger's antics as they watched him play with the kong and a Frisbee morphed into another dinner invitation, and Rex accepted. When Digger resumed his habit of walking between them, he barely noticed. He didn't realize the questions in his mind since the fight in Pattaya were distracting him, because they'd sunk into his subconscious.

Late in the afternoon, Sunstra asked Rex to take her home so she could start some dinner preparations, and suggested he get a little rest because he seemed tired. He hadn't told her about his fight in Pattaya. She'd been so spooked by her own close call that he didn't think it was a great idea to tell her about another one. Besides, he couldn't have told the story without appearing to pat himself on the back for saving the girl. That was the last thing he'd want anyone to take from the story. It wasn't about him—it was about the girl's vulnerability and his worry that she hadn't learned her lesson.

After dropping her off, he went home, took a rare nap, and then a shower to wake himself up. At the time she'd told him to come over, he knocked on her door with a bottle of wine in one hand and a bouquet of colorful flowers in the other.

Sunstra had outdone herself with the meal. Rex had learned proper table manners in Thailand and put no more than two spoonsful of rice on his plate, but he was happy for the dictum that one could go back for more as many times as he wanted. Sunstra kept bringing out dish after dish, reminiscent of Rekha's mother at every meal she'd prepared for him. Each was more delicious than the last, and some were spicy enough to require more than a sip of wine to cool his taste buds.

At the end of the evening, something in Sunstra's eyes led Rex to stand and kiss her, passionately. Digger immediately made his objections known. As the kiss lingered, Digger's growls turned to a bark and he pushed himself between them, quite forcefully.

Rex wasn't drunk, but his inhibitions were definitely lowered, and Sunstra's eager return of the kiss encouraged him. He told her he'd be right back, led Digger out into the hallway, and took a moment to admonish the dog.

"Buddy, you know nothing about human romance. I know you don't have a girlfriend, and you might be jealous because I've got one. But if you want a girl, go find your own. You are not a relationship counselor, either. Now leave me to at least decide who I like and who I don't like. Okay?"

Digger's growl ended with a sharp yelp, but Rex didn't care. He went back inside, shutting the door firmly in Digger's face.

However, his hopes for the evening were dashed when he'd barely taken the first step back to Sunstra before Digger set up a racket. He ignored it, and Digger didn't stop. The neighbors must have gotten fed-up and complained. Not long after, he and Sunstra were interrupted by a knock on the door. When Sunstra opened it, it was an unamused policeman.

Digger was still going on, nonstop.

"You *will* quiet your dog, right now, or we will take him and you into custody," the officer said.

With a regretful glance at Sunstra, Rex stepped forward and took responsibility. "I'm sorry, that's my fault. I'll keep him quiet."

Under the watchful frown of the police, Rex again apologized to Sunstra, took polite leave of her with no physical demonstration, and led Digger away.

Rex was too annoyed and busy with Digger to see the big smile breaking across Sunstra's face as they walked away.

When they were in the tuk-tuk, Rex wasn't as polite when he gave Digger a piece of his mind and let him know he wasn't too pleased with his behavior and the frustrating outcome of what promised to be a very nice and romantic evening—all because of a damn dog who couldn't behave himself.

Digger heard him out, replied with a low growl, turned his head out of the tuk tuk, and lolled his tongue out.

End of conversation.

The next morning, a Sunday, Rex was still annoyed with Digger for his interrupted night with Sunstra, and he had a slight headache from consuming a little more wine than usual. As he ruminated on the events of the previous night, he was confused about Sunstra's mixed messages, and he wondered if she was confused about his.

Rex decided the cure for both his grumpy mood and his

headache would be a nice massage. He cautiously opened his door and looked down the hallway. The coast was clear —Marcel's apartment door was closed. Unfortunately, the coast wasn't completely clear. He and Digger encountered Marcel in the foyer, and there was no way they could avoid him.

Marcel was in full voice, haranguing one of the other residents, a frail-looking older woman, about hiring him to accompany her anywhere she needed to go, so he could protect her. From the look on her face, Rex thought it might be prudent to lure Marcel away from her, before she pulled a sawed-off shotgun from her enormous purse and let Marcel know what she thought of his suggestions.

Sighing with resignation, he called out, "Hey, Marcel, sorry about yesterday."

Marcel turned to him immediately, and the woman sent Rex a grateful glance and scurried away while she had the chance. Marcel barely noticed her departure. He was striding across the foyer floor, his hand outstretched.

"Hi, neighbor! No problem. Let's shake on it."

Rex stretched out his hand and suddenly found himself twisted in a one-eighty, his right forearm and hand flush against his back.

"Digger, OUT," he yelled, just before Marcel would have lost a leg. Rex had at least three ways out of Marcel's grip. All three would have caused him serious injury, the least of which would have been a broken elbow, but it would have been better than the smashed knee or the crashed larynx, come to think of it. The best however, was to just play along for now and not injure the boy.

Digger obeyed, but his tense stance, raised hackles, and vicious growling got Marcel's attention. He let go of Rex and stepped back, his hands up in a gesture of acceptance.

"Hey, no harm, no foul, right? Just a little demo about how friendly-looking people can be dangerous. What's with the dog, man? I wasn't going to hurt you."

Rex quieted Digger and smiled calmly at Marcel. "I understood you wouldn't, but the dog didn't. He's trained to react to threats against me. As you can see, I don't need to know self-defense. I have Digger for that."

"But dude, he may not always be with you. Let me show you just a few moves, seriously."

Rex knew his real feelings about it must have been showing in his eyes. He was having a challenging time restraining himself from bursting into laughter. Only the close call to Marcel, which he didn't seem to even recognize, kept him from doing so.

"No, really, Marcel. I can't stand violence. I don't even watch violent sports. I can barely watch baseball, and basketball is out of the question. All that hitting and shoving, running and diving—not for me. I prefer to watch ballet and listen to opera. Only the non-violent ones, though."

Marcel's jaw dropped. "You can't be serious."

"Yes, I am. That's why I'm here in Thailand—the Land of Smiles— where the people are known to be the friendliest on earth. I just like to visit historical places on my vacations, sort of a busman's holiday, if you know what I mean."

From his blank expression, it was clear Marcel had no idea what the expression meant to practice one's profession even on holiday. Rex didn't enlighten him.

"If you'll excuse me, Marcel, I'm on my way to have a massage. I was driving most of yesterday and the day before; need to get the stress out of my body."

Marcel gave Rex a searching look, apparently still trying to figure out if what he'd said about his favorite pursuits was true. He glanced nervously at Digger, who had stopped growling but continued to stand with barely-restrained tension and stare at him intensely. He took another step back.

"Okay, sure. Sorry. I guess if that's your final answer…"

"It is. I assure you, I'm fine with Digger to protect me. You don't need to worry, but thank you for your concern."

Marcel nodded uncertainly, turned away, and headed out of the foyer. Rex hoped that was the last time he'd have to fend off Marcel's overtures about self-defense.

As soon as they got outside, he started laughing. If he were honest with himself, he was in a better mood than he had been before the encounter. Digger's reaction to Marcel grabbing him was as priceless as it had been dangerous for Marcel. Maybe that's what Digger's reactions to Sunstra touching him were all about. Maybe the dog thought he needed protection. Well, maybe he did.

Chapter Eleven

When they returned to the apartment after his massage, Rex was much more relaxed and in a much better mood. He owed Sunstra an apology for Digger's behavior the night before, so he gave her a call.

They talked for a little while and laughed about Rex's new theory. Sunstra told him she had one of her own.

"Let's compare our theories," she said. "How about lunch?"

"Another picnic?"

"No, let me treat you to an authentic Thai street lunch."

They agreed to meet at a street vendor's booth where she often grabbed a quick lunch between classes. Rex remarked that he was surprised the booth was open on a Sunday, if it was open during the week.

"The owner barely scratches a living from this booth," Sunstra answered, a slight frown indicating her regret that it was so. "He must work every day, and his wife works to prepare the food at home. I've known them for a few years.

It's sad to see how vulnerable they are. Fully half of what they earn goes for protection to corrupt police."

"Why doesn't the government do something about that?"

She looked at him with cynicism in her eyes. "Why would you think the government is less corrupt? Not that I think the government is directly responsible for this man's suffering, but the fact that they are corrupt on so many levels, too busy lining their own pockets to care what happens to the man on the street, so to speak."

Sunstra ordered for them, Pad See Eiw, a dish that consists of wide rice noodles stir-fried in dark soy sauce with chicken, pork, or beef and Chinese cabbage—flavorful, hearty, warm, and comforting. Their dessert was Kluay Tod, a snack made from deep fried mini-bananas prepared in a batter of desiccated coconut and sesame seeds—addictively sweet.

While indulging in their food, Sunstra brought up the topic of Digger's behavior.

"I don't agree with your notion that Digger is jealous of us having a relationship. I did a bit of research about dog psychology, and it seems dogs can be jealous, and they're not hesitant or embarrassed to show it. However, I don't think that's what we're dealing with here."

Rex smiled, "So, Doctor Chevapravatgumrong, what then is your erudite opinion?"

"Hmm, well this might be a bit difficult and awkward to explain. But I think it is probably important to say it..." she hesitated and stared at the table stuttering, "ah... I... I had it all worked out, but now it's difficult to say..."

"What is it, Sunstra? Let it out, no sense in keeping it cooped up."

"Okay." She nodded. "I think Digger is protecting me from you…"

Rex gaped at her, "I… Sunstra, I would never harm you… you must know that by now."

She was shaking her head. "No Ruan, that's not what I mean. I know you would never harm me. But, the thing is, I think Digger knows that you're not ready for a serious relationship. Not that you don't want to have one—oh yes, you certainly want it. So do I, but I've been studying you carefully. You have a battle going on inside you. You've got some unfinished business somewhere. What it is, I have no idea. What I do know is that you're not a university lecturer on sabbatical."

Rex started to protest, but she held up her hand.

"No, let me finish. I'm not going to ask you to tell me who you really are and what you really do for a living. You'll tell me when the time comes or never. You're the type of man I could allow myself to love. With you I would be happy, and I would always feel secure, but—and this is the problem—you're not ready for it. And I think you don't realize it, but Digger does."

Rex was staring at Sunstra's face and eyes. She was not sad, as far as he could tell, she didn't look hurt, which was a relief. While she was talking, he'd realized that she had hit the nail on the head. "And you think Digger senses it?"

She nodded. "That's why he's doing it. In a way, he's protecting me from you. In fact, I think he's protecting us from each other. I'm ready, and you're not. It will never work until we're both ready."

Rex nodded slowly, "You're right, Sunstra. That's what it is. I am not a university lecturer on sabbatical, and I do have unfinished business. Not just that, I've also got some psychological mountains to conquer.

"I'm so sorry, Sunstra. You shouldn't be suffering because I'm all messed up in my head... I..."

She took his hand and looked him straight in the eyes. "Look, we all have our mountains to conquer. But, to do it and succeed we have to be prepared and have to do it at the right time. As far as I am concerned, we're not ready for it, and it's not the right time for it. That might change in the future. In the meantime, there's nothing that prevents us from being friends. Just good friends, which in any event is always a very good basis for any serious romantic relationship."

Rex felt like a mountain had rolled off his shoulders. He raised his glass of Gafa-Yen Lua-mit, a non-alcoholic drink made with iced coffee and rice balls, and said, "To friends."

Sunstra smiled, raised her glass, clinked his in a toast, and said, "To friends."

Below the table, Digger sighed, put his head down on the floor, and closed his eyes to take a nap.

Despite the damper on their afternoon, Rex and Digger enjoyed the rest of the relaxing afternoon with her. Rex and Sunstra agreed on the source of Digger's opposition to their on-again off-again romance, and they agreed they'd had it right the first time they'd discussed it—they should just be friends. Maybe Digger knew something they didn't.

———

Rex and Digger were returning to the apartment when Rex spotted Marcel running toward them as he pulled into the parking garage. He'd barely stopped when Marcel ran up to him, his eyes wide with fear and shock. His nose was bleeding, and his right eye was beginning to swell shut.

"Quick, take me out of here! They're going to kill me!"

It was a very different Marcel from the cocky kid Rex had met earlier in the day.

He kept his voice level and his expression neutral as he said, "What's going on? Who's going to kill you?"

Marcel's voice was high-pitched as the story tumbled out so fast that Rex had trouble following. "Some guy was dissing me outside the bar last night. I taught him a lesson, broke his arm, I guess. I took off before the cops could get there. But when I got to my gym this afternoon, the guy's brothers were waiting for me. They're masters of Muay Thai! They started whaling on me, and I got away, but they're after me. Come on, dude, let's move!"

Rex would have preferred to get more explanation, but Marcel was so worked up that Rex started to back the tuk-tuk out of his parking space. However, it was too late. He hadn't fully cleared the space before three young men, bigger than the average Thai, appeared in his rear-view mirror. He stopped, pulled the tuk-tuk forward again, and stepped out, facing them. Behind them stood a fourth person, the younger, smaller kid, his arm in a cast, and his face badly bruised. He looked to be about half Marcel's size.

Before Rex could speak to the men, Marcel stepped in front of him. "Get out. This isn't your fight. I'm as good as dead, but I'll stay and fight to the end, to give you a chance to get away. You'd better run while you can. Call the cops."

Rex stepped around him calmly, Digger keeping pace, and approached the brothers. For a few paces, Marcel kept trying to get in front, protesting all the time that he'd do the fighting, and Rex should get away and call the police.

Rex never took his eyes off the brothers. He brushed Marcel gently out of the way, and Marcel gave up before they drew too near the brothers. Rex continued until he and

Digger were within a few feet. Not too near, to respect their personal boundaries, not so far that he had to raise his voice to speak to them in the echoey garage.

"What seems to be the problem, men?" he said, in perfect, unaccented Thai.

Their expressions remained stony, though he thought they may have been surprised to be addressed by a *farang* in that way.

Brother number one, the biggest, and by the looks of it the oldest, who was still smaller than Rex, spoke up, his tone surly. "No talk. Get out of the way. Our quarrel is with him." He pointed at Marcel by lifting his chin in Marcel's direction.

Rex stood his ground. "I understand you're angry. I'll talk to my friend and ask him to apologize and pay your brother's medical bill. It doesn't excuse his behavior, but what's done is done. Beating him up will not unbreak your brother's arm."

"No, we're going to break his arm. That is our right. Move aside, or you will make enemies of us, too."

Rex shook his head regretfully. "I'm sorry, but I can't let you do that. I'm sorry he hurt your brother, and I can make him give restitution. Revenge isn't an option, though."

In the convex mirror above the brothers' heads, placed there to help drivers see other vehicles in the parking area and avoid accidents, Rex could see that Marcel was agitated. He was gesticulating and shouting in English, posing in *katas*, breathing loudly, and generally making a fool of himself. Rex noted that, though Marcel was yelling at him to let him handle it, he did so from the safe distance of five or more yards away.

At Rex's side, Digger sat facing toward him, looking back and forth between Marcel and the threat, as if he couldn't decide what to do about all this. Rex caught the tilt of his head when he was watching Marcel's antics. Marcel was no threat, so Rex ignored him and very quietly said "Cover" to Digger. At that, Digger turned around and faced the threatening brothers.

Rex hadn't told Digger to attack in any way, so he remained relaxed, not quite smiling his happy dog smile, but not growling, either. One of the brothers was keeping a wary eye on the dog.

Rex tried once more. "Guys, listen to me. You don't want to mess with us. Stand down, and let's talk like adults. No one has to get hurt."

Brother number one shook his head. Rex saw that the détente was over.

He hand-signaled Digger to threaten, and from the corner of his eye he saw Digger's haunches come up. He knew Digger would be drawing his lips back and showing his teeth in a clear signal that the brothers should rather walk away.

Evidently, they didn't understand dog language.

He hadn't finished the last word before the answer came. It was not verbal. Brother one had decided the talking was over and made his move, but before he moved, he telegraphed his intention to Rex by a look in his eye. With a wild swing, he covered the few feet between them. Rex was ready with a block. He stepped aside and swept the attacker's legs out from under him, dumping him on his ass.

Rex had no time to check the first brother's status, as brother number two was stepping up to the plate already, faking a punch to Rex's head while going for a kick to his ribs. Rex ignored the fake, correctly surmising that the kick was the real threat. Instead of backing away from it, he surprised brother two and stepped into it, robbing it of its power. He grabbed the guy's knee and lifted it straight up, at the same time pushing back. Brother two went down on his back, but both he and brother one powered themselves back to their feet with a gymnastic move and rushed Rex.

The brother who'd been watching Digger took his eyes off the dog and made a move to join the fray, but Digger jumped between him and the others. He growled and barked a short, sharp warning. Brother three got the message and backed away, standing close to his injured younger brother.

Digger sat to watch them with no further threat.

Rex didn't want to hurt the men. They had a legitimate beef with Marcel, and he was going to straighten things out with the brat as soon as this was over. However, he didn't plan to get himself hurt in the process. So he fell back on Tai Chi moves, blocking and defending but not attacking. Every chance he got, he emphasized his points by kicking them in the ass, but not too hard, or slapping them open-handed against their heads when their defenses failed to protect them.

It didn't take them long to get the message that they were outclassed, and that it was obvious this man was capable of seriously harming them if they continued to attack and annoyed him enough. As if they'd discussed it beforehand, both brothers stopped attacking. They stepped back, standing side-by-side, and bowed formally to him, as if to a sensei in a dojo.

As soon as they stopped, Rex stood upright, dropped his defensive stance, and called to Marcel to come and join him. He didn't look back to see the approach, but he could see in the mirror that Marcel was coming.

As soon as he felt the kid's presence at his side, he said, still without looking, "You owe that boy an apology. Say it to him and then to his brothers. Say it loud—I want to hear you, and they must hear you. Also tell them you'll be paying for the kid's medical expenses."

Marcel opened his mouth to protest, but Digger warned him with a growl that he was on probation. Marcel said a few words of reluctant apology, and Rex translated, making it more gracious than it had been. If the brothers spoke English, which he suspected they probably did, they'd know he'd cleaned up the apology, but it didn't matter.

When Marcel was done, Rex sternly told the brothers they should accept and shake hands. "Don't make any moves out of the handshakes, or we'll finish what we started here."

Reluctantly, they shook Marcel's hand and gave him artificial smiles.

Rex asked Marcel if he had any cash on him and got a sullen no for an answer.

"Go get some, at least one thousand bhat. We'll be waiting for your return. Don't make me wait too long."

As soon as Marcel left, the brothers broke into genuine smiles and crowded around Rex. Digger tensed, but a hand signal from Rex settled him down.

As before, the oldest and biggest brother was the spokesman. He was effusive in his praise of Rex and his moves, saying they'd never seen anyone move like him or defend like that, and they wanted to know more.

"Let us buy you a beer. Maybe you can teach us your moves. We'll pay you well and arrange as many beautiful girls for you as you desire."

Rex politely declined and was secretly relieved when Marcel returned with the money. He said maybe another time for the beer and definitely no thank you for the offer of girls. The biggest brother took possession of the money and led the others out of the garage.

Marcel started to leave as well, but he halted quickly when Rex took hold of his ear like he would a naughty kid.

"Ow! What the hell, man?"

"First, don't let me ever hear of you bullying a younger, smaller kid again. Got that?"

"Yes."

"Good. Second, if you ever tell anyone what you saw today, I will personally deliver you to those guys and tell them you said their mother had sex with mules. You got that?"

Marcel nodded painfully, swiping ineffectually at Rex's strong fingers on his ear. "I've got it. Jeez, let go, man. You could have told me you could handle yourself."

Digger didn't like his tone. He growled, and Marcel shut up for once. Rex let his ear go, and Marcel jogged away without looking back.

Two days later, Rex saw a For-Rent sign on Marcel's door. He hoped the kid had gone to India to learn about meditation and inner peace. He didn't have much hope for the kid's acting career. He wouldn't make a good action hero star, but maybe he could try for a role as a porn star.

But what do I know about acting?

It was the day after he noticed the For-Rent sign that he heard from Sunstra again. She wanted to meet him for an ice cream that afternoon. Rex gladly agreed.

When they met, he noticed she was troubled about something and assumed she'd tell him what it was, but all she said was that she was leaving for a while to visit her parents. She then asked if he'd like to join her in Phuket the following Friday, and she'd show him the sights. They agreed on a time and place, and she air-kissed his cheek when she left.

Chapter Twelve

Josh and Marissa were thorough in their search for Bruce Carson. They had a semi-cold lead from Brandt, who'd seen Carson board the plane for the Marshall Islands and had watched until the plane took off. However, that had been weeks ago. Rather than taking off in a rush on what could be another fruitless physical search, they brainstormed an approach and decided it was prudent to set an electronic search in motion first.

Carson had been head of the CIA and the last link in a chain of corruption that led to the betrayal of Rex Dalton and his team in Afghanistan. With his disappearance, a new CIA head had been appointed, but John Brandt hadn't trusted him with every bit of intelligence he had. Trusting political appointees, such as the Director of the CIA, was just not his style.

The primary directive in a search for a person with financial resources was 'follow the money'. Carson had never been a field agent, or spook, as they were known. He'd joined the CIA directly out of college and became an analyst of European affairs. Throughout his career he did everything expected of a career bureaucrat, in other words, he kept his head down in a crisis, attended social events to rub shoulders with the elite, and kept his sights fixed on the top job. It worked. A few decades of doing that and he was considered an experienced administrator and a safe bet for a President who didn't want to be embarrassed.

Although Carson lacked the skills of a real spy, he had the sophistication to make his money vanish, and so he had. Before leaving the US, he'd wiped out every penny in his accounts, leaving his wife near-destitute and mad as the proverbial wet hen, not to mention the fury when she discovered that no one wanted to believe that she was not in cahoots with her deviant husband. She was more than happy to cooperate when Josh and Marissa contacted her for more information, expressing the explicit desire to be allowed to put her hands around his neck and throttle all life out of him if they found him.

Unfortunately, her information didn't do that much good. She gave them everything she had, which was access to the empty accounts, but even the banks and investment account organizations couldn't tell them with certainty where the money went when it left their control. There were hints, of course. Obviously, the recipient accounts were located in countries with strict privacy laws. That's where Brandt's Finint prodigies came in. They started working on breaking through the layers of secrecy to follow that trail.

Carson must have developed secret resources among some of the CIA employees. The second prong of the attack was to suss out those human resources and grill them for information as to Carson's current whereabouts. But it took time, and time was what America's spy agencies didn't have. They'd already lost a couple of good assets and had one long-term operation blown wide open, requiring them to pull out their field agents and end the mission. Carson was out there somewhere selling his secrets.

Once again delegating the task of unraveling Carson's network, Josh and Marissa moved on to the final leg of the three-pronged attack: Sigint. Somehow, Carson was staying in touch with his resources, and he was also in touch with enemy agencies. They had to surmise he was also in touch with the middle link in the chain Rex Dalton had been trying to break: the drug trade from Afghanistan to the US. The snake had been decapitated with the raid on Usama's compound, when the major drug lords in Afghanistan were all killed. Whether that was the work of Rex Dalton or not was not relevant for now. The issue was that this snake was like the multi-headed Hydra of lore. It was already sprouting new heads.

The elderly Senator who'd controlled Carson had committed suicide, thus breaking the chain from that end. It was obvious someone was still controlling both ends of the drug trade between the US and Afghanistan from the middle, and it wasn't out of the question that Carson was in touch with that someone. If they could figure out who this was and monitor the person's communications, it could also lead to Carson. But the first thing required to prove that hypothesis was a name—given the urgency, it was regarded as another dead end, for now.

They considered the next option—modern travel was such that one could usually track someone's movements with enough money, coercion, or diplomacy. With every-thing else delegated, Josh and Marissa started on that. They knew Carson had flown to the Marshall Islands, and they knew why. The Marshall Islands, while enjoying a good relationship with the US, did not have an extradition treaty.

He would have had time and the financial resources to move freely about the islands. Discovering where he'd gone from his initial destination would require that in-person search after all.

It didn't take much to learn there were thirty airports on the various islands, excluding the three military airports they assumed he wouldn't use. Carson's flight had been bound for Marshall Islands International Airport on Majuro Atoll. From there, he could have puddle-jumped for as long as he wished, before leaving the tiny country of a little more than fifty-thousand people, bound for anywhere.

It could take weeks to get a fresher lead, but that was nothing new. They'd experienced that in Afghanistan and India, looking for Rex. They could only hope Carson hadn't learned somewhere how to stay hidden. With backup of the combined skills of CRC and CIA Finint, Humint, and Sigint experts, their efforts this time would hopefully bear fruit. They departed for the Marshall Islands within a few days of getting the assignment.

Sometimes it was Josh's boyish good looks and charm, and sometimes it was Marissa's beauty that opened the doors. In this case it could have been a combination of those factors that got them much more cooperation from local employees of the airlines and airports than any official channels had produced prior to their arrival. Carson had peculiar and specialized tastes in 'entertainment', as Marissa delicately called the pervert's vulgar habits. Questioning the airline staff at the first airport, they were told some remembered him because he asked openly where he could find such entertainment.

The two of them followed his trail, from airport to private club or brothel to the next airport. It turned out he'd visited only three of the twenty-nine atolls, before departing for New Zealand about ten days after he'd arrived.

Josh and Marissa flew to Auckland, New Zealand and took up the search with the same methods as before. However, before they could get a bead on his travels, word from back home was the IT folks at Sigint had picked up the trail from there. Of all the stupid things he could have done, Carson was using his own identity and his passport to travel. Maybe he was in too much of a hurry to find a forger to change identities before he left the US. That was understandable—if John Brandt, the CEO of CRC, gives you twenty-four hours to disappear or die, you'd be in a hurry to pack and leave—unless you had a death wish.

Brandt checked with his CIA contact and verified that Carson hadn't had access to any CIA-produced false papers. That made it easier. The trail led to Samoa, where it went cold temporarily. But Josh and Marissa managed to find the forger who'd supplied Carson's new identity, and they followed that to Chile.

"Just like a damn Nazi war criminal." Josh joked.

"Maybe not as directly responsible for millions of lives lost," Marissa answered more soberly, "but still responsible for everyone who's lost their life to drug overdose or the crap the street dealers cut the drugs with, since he became involved. Not to mention Rex's team and maybe Rex himself. Let's go get the son of a bitch."

Josh shook his head. "Marissa, the guy knows you. I'd better go on my own."

She started to protest but then realized that though she would have liked to take a piece of Carson's hide out with her own two hands, it was far too important to risk their target spotting them and bolting.

She flew home from Samoa, while Josh continued to Santiago.

It was the first time they'd been apart in weeks. Josh wasn't sure how Marissa felt about it, but he felt like he'd lost an arm or something. They worked so well together, and they completed each other in many ways. However, he had a job to do, and the sooner he did it, the sooner he could get home and resume the search for Rex Dalton—with Marissa.

Cooperation from back home helped him track Carson, now traveling as Barclay Cooper, from Santiago to Valparaiso, about sixty miles away. When Josh got there, he wished Marissa was still with him. The beautiful city was built upon dozens of steep hillsides. It had been declared a World Heritage Site by UNESCO a dozen or so years before, which had led to preservation of the unique funicular system of public transport. National monuments of historical significance abounded among colorfully painted houses that lent a fresh and whimsical vibe to the city.

Marissa would have loved it.

With his new identity and his ill-gotten gains from the drug trade in the form of a mountain of cash, Carson had established a home in the penthouse of a luxury apartment building at the apex of one of the tallest hills. With surveillance, Josh learned that Carson evidently didn't feel the need for bodyguards, probably because he lived in the illusion that he had pulled a David Seth Kotkin, better known by his stage name David Copperfield, on the CIA and the world.

What an idiot. He of all people should know better.

Josh didn't feel the need to give him any advice on the matter. He simply rang the doorbell one afternoon after he'd spent a few days in observation. A pretty Chilean woman in an old-fashioned maid's uniform opened the door. Her expression was carefully schooled to be pleasant, but under her makeup, Josh could see the shadow of a bruise around her left eye. Her demeanor was subservient.

Josh had to use a bit of schooling himself not to react to what he immediately assumed was abuse of this woman, probably by Carson himself, knowing his predilections. Without saying a word, he promised the woman her injuries would be avenged, but his voice didn't betray it as he asked for Señor Cooper and was admitted to the house.

Josh cooled his heels but not his temper as he waited in the parlor while the maid summoned Carson. In only a few minutes, Carson appeared, affable and willing to entertain this drop-in guest. His demeanor didn't last long.

"Mr. Carson, I've been sent to bring you back to the United States. Come along peacefully, and everything will be all right." Josh let his jacket open just enough for Carson to see the Sig Sauer, courtesy of a CIA plant in the embassy in Santiago, thrust into his waistband.

At first, Carson tried to bluff. "I'm afraid you're mistaken about my identity," he said, trying with little success to appear calm.

"I'm afraid you've mistaken me for an idiot," Josh said in a measured tone. "Have your help pack a suitcase for you, and we'll be on our way."

Emboldened by the fact that Josh hadn't shown him a badge or anything to indicate official status, Carson did relax. His expression morphed from slightly nervous to supercilious.

"I don't think so. You have no status, or you'd have arrested me. Get out."

Josh smiled. "Here's my status," he said as he drew the Sig with the silencer fitted to the end. "Call the woman and tell her to pack your stuff."

The blood had drained from Carson's face and he slowly raised his hands.

Josh could see the wheels turning in Carson's head. *Anxious people can make stupid moves.* He leveled the pistol at Carson's head and hardened his gaze.

"You know I can't return to the States. I don't know who you are, or who sent you, but I'd guess you're a bounty hunter. I can pay you. Name your price."

Josh stayed silent, and Carson seemed to deflate, dropping the arrogance.

"Please. My life in the US is over, I can never set foot there again. My wife is divorcing me, my reputation is ruined. I can't go to prison... they'll... I'll never... Why can't you just be satisfied that I'm no longer in a position to do any damage?"

Josh's hard demeanor cracked. His jaw dropped, and he felt fury overtake him. "No damage? *No damage!* You sanctimonious son of a bitch. You've gotten three good agents and several of their local assets killed. You've destroyed a couple of million dollars' worth of operations that had to be dropped when you exposed them, and you're directly responsible for killing a good friend of mine and his team in an ambush in Afghanistan. *No damage.* You say that one more time and I'll shoot you where you stand."

Carson had been impassive against the accusations until Josh mentioned his friend and his team. Then his face went ashen. "You're CRC?"

"Damn straight and proud of it. Just an FYI about my

brief, I've been ordered to take you back to the US alive but have been authorized to terminate you if that's not possible. And one thing you might not know about me—I've never failed to complete an assignment."

Carson's shoulders slumped. "All right. Don't shoot—I just need to call Maria on the intercom." He gestured toward a corner of the room.

Josh nodded, keeping his weapon trained on Carson as he turned and took a step toward the table in the corner with what looked like a telephone on it. Josh had let his eyes stray toward the corner for half a second, so he missed it when Carson's muscles bunched. He turned the gun and squeezed the trigger as Carson made a leap for the window, and he thought he saw the round hit home, but before he could process what he'd seen, Carson's body had plummeted the ten stories to the steep hillside below.

In shock, Josh rushed to the window to try to spot the body. There was too much greenery below. He needed to get down there in case there was any way Carson had survived, finish him off, and get out of town. Already he could hear Maria screaming in another room. He dashed back to the passage from the parlor to the front door, passing her on the way. In hurried Spanish, he said there'd been an accident.

It was the best he could do for her. His quick observation of the broken window convinced him the death could be ruled suicide if he'd missed Carson and no bullet could be found. There was no blood on the window.

The next moment, the maid burst into the room, saw the broken window, and then her eyes darted around and found no Carson. She broke down in hysteria. Josh was sure she couldn't have heard the shot, and she couldn't have seen anything because she was in another room, but if the body showed a gunshot, he'd have to get rid of it, quickly.

What a snafu! Damn, *I wish Marissa were here. I could use some help.*

Twenty-four hours later, Josh and Marissa stood on the carpet in Brandt's DC office. Josh had located Carson's body, and it was battered and scratched from his fall through the trees and into the garden below. He hadn't found a bullet wound, concluding that maybe one of the scratches on his neck and shoulders had been from a graze by his shot but would not be easy to pick up by the coroner —the cause of death was obviously not a bullet wound.

Josh firmly believed he couldn't have missed altogether, but The Old Man was having a field day dressing him down for both Carson's suicide and his wild shot.

"I can't believe it. Shit, what did you learn during training? Rule number one about guns—CRC agents are not gangsters—we don't go around brandishing guns and threatening people with them. CRC agents draw their guns for one reason and one reason only, to kill someone. Rule number two, a CRC agent never misses."

In the silence that followed, the Old Man sighed and shrugged before he continued. "But I guess it could have been a lot worse, Farley. You were lucky to have missed or almost missed."

But after saying that, he couldn't help himself and continued his rant. "Damn, just listen to me, I can't believe I am even saying it, 'lucky that you missed or almost missed'."

At that Josh started to relax.

Brandt saw it and started again, "Don't you relax yet, boy. You could've done a lot better. You do realize that thanks to you falling asleep on the job we're fresh out of leads now. He might have told us the name of the drug mastermind here in the US, if we could have questioned him. And he might have had an idea whether Rex is dead or alive."

Josh hung his head. "Yes, sir. I'm sorry."

"Yeah, yeah I know, and it won't happen again and all that BS. Go get yourself something to eat and get some sleep. Be back here in the morning."

Josh nodded and left without another word to either Brandt or Marissa. He just smiled as he left the office. They all knew the Old Man, he always had this hard-baked, bombastic way about him, but everyone knew he cared as much for his agents as he would've cared for his own children, if he had any.

Marissa laughed.

"Why are you laughing?" Brandt snapped.

"I'm wondering if Josh knows that all your ranting just now was actually not as serious as it sounded and that you're actually kind of happy with the outcome?"

"Yeah well, my agents don't have to know when I'm serious or not," he grumbled.

"But I would've liked for us to have had a chance to interrogate Carson."

"Leadership a la John Brandt style, I guess," Marissa replied with a sweet smile.

"Okay, Josh is overdue for R and R. What about you? Do you need a break?"

She thought for a moment. "I don't *need* one, but I wouldn't object to one. What would you say if we took it together, Josh and me?"

"So that's the way it is?"

"Maybe it is, maybe it's not, who knows?" She grinned. "But we *do* enjoy each other's company. If we're not violating some rule you haven't told me about."

"So, if it's against the rules, does that mean you'll stop enjoying each other's company?"

"Yeah, I guess if you want to issue an order to that effect, we'll stop enjoying it."

Brandt suppressed a smile when the thought crossed his mind that if he had a daughter, this is exactly what she would be like. "Okay, in that case you're ordered to keep on enjoying each other's company, so long as it doesn't interfere with your performance. Is that clear?"

"Yes, sir. Clear as mother's milk, sir." She smiled as she mock-saluted him.

"Okay – you two take a month and make sure you come back sharp."

"Thanks, John. See you in a month," she said as she got up and left to find Josh.

Chapter Thirteen

Despite their agreement to just be friends, Rex missed Sunstra's company during the following week. She'd gone to Phuket to visit her parents, and he'd spent the week doing day trips into the countryside around Bangkok, talking to old people he met about their memories of WWII. Those who remembered much were in their late eighties, and often they waved him away, saying they'd rather not talk about it.

Thailand's position during the war had been that of a reluctant ally of Japan. They'd been invaded, and the prime minister had elected to cooperate rather than fight. Subsequent bombing raids by Allied forces on Bangkok had strengthened dissatisfaction with him, and his successor had continued a charade of collaboration while shielding the growing underground movement. The movement was preparing an assault on Japanese forces when Japan's surrender occurred.

Everyone willing to talk to Rex claimed to be part of the underground, even those who would have been young teens at the time. He considered it a largely wasted week, and he was heartily looking forward to a pleasant weekend with Sunstra as he boarded a plane to Phuket on Thursday afternoon.

He'd considered driving. The journey would have taken him down the long peninsula on the west side of the Gulf of Thailand toward Malaysia, but there were few towns of interest to him along the five-hundred-mile journey. Almost eleven hours in the driver's seat, and long stretches where there'd be nowhere to get something to eat or fill up the gas tank—not his favorite choice.

He apologized to Digger for his sojourn in the cargo hold of the plane, but it would be for only a little over an hour. Digger didn't seem to mind, even when Rex ordered him into the wire cage he was required to travel in. Digger even looked a bit excited, as if he knew that some kind of new adventure awaited him.

The dog was more than glad to see him at the other end of the trip, though. He frolicked like a puppy when Rex let him out of the cage. Rex promised him a run in the first park they came to while he waited in line to get the keys to his rental car. They had the evening and night to kill before they picked up Sunstra at her parents' house for breakfast the next morning. Rex kept his promise and let Digger play to his heart's content in a park, then drove about twenty miles to Sunstra's parent's neighborhood on the west side of the island to be sure of his directions before checking into his hotel. He hoped she'd introduce him and maybe give him a tour of the grounds before they went out. The neighborhood was close to the beach, and he could catch tantalizing glimpses of the sea between the bungalows. Phuket was actually an island, with a narrow sound separating it from the mainland. Beyond the beaches, the Andaman Sea stretched toward the Indian Ocean.

Rex expected Sunstra to show him the sights, so rather than exploring on his own that night, he and Digger had a quiet evening, relying on room service for their dinner and turning in early to be up early the next morning.

So, it was that Rex was soundly sleeping when the sirens started.

Digger had heard them before Rex did, maybe a function of the high pitch as they started sounding with the eerie wee-wa, wee-wa Rex associated with European police sirens. Digger's howl joined the sirens to startle Rex out of sleep, leaping out of bed before he was fully awake.

What the hell?

He couldn't help but recall the sounds of the sirens on that fateful morning at Atocha Station, Madrid, Spain on March 11, 2004 after the al Qaeda bomb explosions killed his entire family.

He reached for the phone to call down to the front desk and ask what was going on, but before he found it in the dark, he heard a loudspeaker. Between the sirens and Digger's mournful howling, he couldn't understand the words.

"Digger, quiet."

Digger gave him a reproachful look but stopped his infernal howling. Instead, he crept under the bed on his belly, shivering and whining quietly. Rex sympathised—the sirens were disturbing him, too. As whatever was carrying the loudspeaker came closer, he could barely make out the words, which were being repeated in Thai and English. He finally caught the most important word. Tsunami!

Rex listened more closely as he switched on the light and reached for his pants. The early-warning system had partially done its job. They were being warned. The problem was that the first high waves were expected in only an hour. Everyone was warned to get to high ground.

This is a disaster in the making. Rapid evacuation makes for careless driving. People are going to get hurt.

Even as he assessed the situation, Rex was pulling on his clothes and shoes, reassuring Digger that the sirens would soon stop, though he knew they wouldn't, and calling to the front desk for his car to be brought around. He offered to ferry a couple of guests in the hotel without a car if they could be ready when the car got there.

He checked the room for anything he couldn't afford to lose, stuffed his wallet and passport in his pockets, put Digger's collar and leash on him, and left, less than two minutes after he'd been awakened.

Downstairs, he found half a dozen people waiting for him. He shook his head, dismayed. He only had room for two if he took Digger, and though he might later be criticized for it, there was no way on God's earth that he was going to leave Digger behind. He pointed at two women, an American pleading in Southern-accented English and her teen-aged daughter.

"I can take you two. I'll come back for the rest of you if I can."

"But my husband! Leave your dog behind."

"No can do. If you don't want the seats, I'll take two others."

"Go on, honey," a man standing by her said. "I'll get another ride. Get Samantha to safety."

It was only when he'd dropped them off, two miles away at the top of a rise where evacuees were gathering, and he was heading back to the hotel for more, that he realized he should be heading west, toward Sunstra. Her neighborhood was about to be hit!

He looked at his watch. The loudspeakers that woke him said there was only an hour to evacuate. That had been half an hour ago, and Sunstra and her parents were about half an hour to the west, in the direction of the tsunami. He could make it, if he didn't return to the hotel. He made a sharp turn and headed for Sunstra's at speeds the road was never meant for, dodging cars and bikes headed his way in the same manner.

Rex wasn't worried about being stopped for speeding. He reckoned every cop in the city was engaged in the evacuation effort. However, he kept one hand on the horn as he sped along. Poor Digger was in agony with the sounds of the sirens and the horn. He lay on the floor below the back seat, whimpering and occasionally adding a thin howl to the mix, as if he were trying to whisper it.

Ten minutes later, Rex reached the outskirts of the city and stepped on the accelerator.

The traffic was lighter—alarmingly so.

Had the villages to the west not been notified of the tsunami? Or had they gotten even earlier warning and now everyone was already out? Without knowing which, Rex couldn't take the chance it wasn't the former. He had to get to Sunstra and her family.

He drove farther and rounded a curve a couple of minutes later and noticed that the road was wet—it distressed him.

Am I too late?

Ahead, he could see flashing lights. He slowed only a little, but when he got just a little closer, he could see there was a barrier across the road. He came to a stop, and a policeman quickly walked to his window.

"Turn around. Not safe," the policeman ordered. He

119

spoke English, apparently deciding Rex wasn't Thai. Rex answered in Thai.

"My friend and her family live near the beach. Did they get notification? Are they out? I can beat the wave and get them to safety."

"You cannot beat the wave. It is here."

He leaned out the window and saw the road was awash, and the water rapidly getting deeper. As he watched, it crept up toward the car's hubcaps.

If he didn't turn around, his engine would soon be flooded.

"I'll turn around. Can I give you a ride to safety?"

"It is safe here for a few more minutes but not farther down the road. I have a vehicle and will be leaving soon. I regret to tell you that the warning did not come in time for everyone. Maybe your friends evacuated. Maybe not. You must return to Phuket now."

Rex turned the car around and headed back to the city, his chest tight and his stomach sour. The land sloped down-ward toward the beach where Sunstra's family lived. Even right there at the road barrier, it was little more than a few feet above sea level. From what he knew of tsunamis, the first indication might have been a drawback, but because it was the middle of the night, who would have been there to see it? And how much time would they have had to respond before the full wave hit? Ten minutes, at most, and that was from the time the drawback started, if in fact there'd been one. There might have been no warning at all.

Rex knew the worst-hit area in the tsunami of 2004 was somewhere north of Phuket. 2004 had been a bad year for Rex, and he'd barely noticed the news of the tsunami then. He knew more about it from his recent research.

As he drove toward Phuket, Rex talked himself into

believing that Sunstra and her family were just fine. The massive wave would have affected parts north more than her beach, and besides, those bungalows were up on stilts. He searched his memory for images of hers he'd seen the day before. All he could recall was the image of peeks of snow-white sands between the houses.

Despite the disturbing thoughts, he noticed the water keeping pace with him as he drove back to the east. When a curve that had hidden the road barrier from him as he drove west came up, his steering wheel wasn't as responsive. Turning was a chore. He rolled down the window and stuck his head outside. The water was now well over the hubcaps and still rising, and for the next few miles, his route was parallel to the sea!

Sparing a fleeting thought for the safety of the cop who'd turned him back, Rex pushed the gas pedal to the floor, hoping against hope he could reach the spot where the road curved back to the west before the car was washed off the road.

"Hang on, Digger. Let's hope we don't have to swim for safety."

Driving forward as fast as the vehicle could go with a massive amount of water pushing him sideways took all Rex's skill and concentration. At times, he wasn't certain he was on the road or even that the wheels were in contact with solid ground, though they must have been. He overshot the curve and was thrown forward when the front wheels hit mud, but he was able to turn the wheels and regain the road. Now he had the momentum of the wave itself pushing him faster than he could have gone with just the car's own power. It was looking like he'd made a grave error in trying to get to Sunstra.

He and Digger might lose their own lives.

Eight more excruciating minutes brought him to the city, where the wave was impeded and broken up by buildings. He breathed a sigh of relief and followed directions of the police, who were at every corner it seemed, directing traffic to higher ground. He found the rise where the other guests from his hotel were huddled. Unsure of his welcome, he parked the car where he was told and got out to stand beside it.

The sirens had stopped, thankfully. Rex coaxed Digger out of the car, clipped his leash on, and kept his hand on the shaggy back, reassuring the dog they were both okay and the danger had passed. Digger was a brave dog, Rex had no doubt of that. He'd charge a man with a gun to save his human partner, but he'd never encountered a situation like this before. There was no discernable enemy, only painful noises and shouting and Rex's tension, which the dog would feel as if it were his own.

No wonder he's terrified.

"It's okay, buddy," Rex said aloud. "We're okay, and I can only pray Sunstra is, too."

Digger lifted his ears at Sunstra's name, but he didn't stop shivering.

I'm unsure she's okay, and he can feel it.

Chapter Fourteen

While Josh and Marissa were gone for their R and R break, Brandt had returned to picking threads from information he'd received after Rex's assumed death.

He always had plenty to do, between recruiting and supervising the training of new recruits and overseeing ongoing missions of his teams. More work came to them than they could take on, but he sometimes felt it necessary to go and schmooze with those of his clients who valued political BS. However, with two of his best agents on leave, there were holes in his day he was constitutionally unable to leave for mere relaxation. He spent them combing news and intelligence reports for any hint that someone like Rex was operating on his own, somewhere.

Call it intuition or call it being attuned to the best agent he'd ever had, the man he'd thought of as a true son. His thoughts kept turning to the odd story out of Saudi Arabia a few weeks after Rex's presumed death. He'd always been sceptical about one man operating on his own with no support team behind him taking out a Saudi prince and his entire security team and still managing to escape.

Unreal as the whole story may have sounded, he'd never known anyone else but Rex Dalton who had the brains and guts capable of pulling off a stunt as audacious as that one. In the past, he'd reluctantly dismissed it as a clue, mainly because of the report of a big black dog being involved. Rex had no dog handler skills, but he couldn't stop wondering.

With nothing but his strong feeling that Rex was alive and the lack of other clues behind it, he finally decided he had to settle the matter once and for all. Was the Saudi's death at Rex's hands, or not? However, he couldn't just send Josh and Marissa to Saudi Arabia without something more to go on. So, before they returned, he'd need to get more.

But how? The answer was to dance delicately along the strings of international cooperation between secret agencies, some of which were usually reluctant to cooperate but occasionally did. His only entrance to that world was by twitching his strings to the CIA with the intention of eventually getting the truth, the *whole* truth, out of the Mabahith, the Saudi Secret police.

He made a call to a former colleague, someone he'd worked with during his CIA career and still working at the CIA, but who wasn't interested in a political rise. It wouldn't do to dissemble with this man. He'd smell a line of bullshit a mile away. So, Brandt laid his cards on the table. He appealed to his friend's feelings for his own boy, recently recruited to the CIA over his father's objections. The friend agreed to help.

A few days later, the friend called from a secure phone. "Okay, here's the scoop. I have an asset in the Saudi General Intelligence Presidency, okay? And if I ever hear that anyone else knows it, I'll kill you, bury you in your beloved desert, and tell God you just died. Got it?"

Brandt laughed. "I think I have the picture. But you know that wasn't necessary. I'd never…"

"Just a precaution. I'm a cautious man." The friend lowered his voice. "Next caveat. You now owe me. If my boy gets into any kind of trouble, anywhere, you'll send your best team, at no cost, to get him out."

"Done." Knowing his friend, Brandt had little expectation of having to pay up on that one. If the boy was as good as his father, there'd be no need.

"So, my asset leaned on an asset of *his*, in Mabahith. From here, the story gets really strange."

"Go on, I'm all ears," Brandt urged.

A week later, two days after they returned from R and R, Brandt met with Josh and Marissa, looking tan and refreshed, at his DC office.

"Strange how?" Marissa prompted when he got to that part of the story.

"Well, only the part about the dog. It could have been a djinn," he said, unsmiling.

"What?!" Josh and Marissa exclaimed in unison.

"Let me back up. So, this Mutaib, the Saudi prince, was a known illegal arms dealer, but his status as part of the royal family protected him, right? However, he was an embarrassment to the King, so the official investigation didn't go far. It was the Mabahith that dug for details, and then buried them again.

"It seems the guy had an official and an unofficial harem. Apparently, that's not unusual. What's strange is that when this operative, whoever it was, raided the guy's residence, he killed Mutaib, all his guards, and took some valuables, along with half his harem—the unofficial half. Well, not all of them, but most of them. Seven women and a little girl. And apparently the dog, or djinn, whatever it was, helped. Climbed a tree to get into the compound, if you can believe that."

Marissa was shaking her head. "Why are you interested in this, John?"

"It could have been Rex. Do you know of anyone else, ours or internationally, that could have pulled that off?"

Marissa waved her hand in a dismissive gesture. "No, I've never met Rex, I only know what you and Josh told me about him. Admittedly, by all accounts, Dalton seems to be a very capable man. But let's be realistic, this is not Hollywood. Djinn? Are you serious? C'mon John, this is a fairy tale. It's been exaggerated by the witnesses to absolve them of any blame.

"Why would Rex have been involved in something like that? If he's alive, and you know that's a big if, he'd be hiding. For what reason on earth would he get involved in a high-profile crime in a country where getting caught would mean a death sentence? Why would he abduct a bunch of civilians, and maybe get them killed too? It doesn't make sense."

Josh wasn't so sure. "Well, look. Rex Dalton specialized in the impossible. Remember London? And come to think of it Naples and..."

Brandt held his hand up to stop Josh and brought Marissa up to speed on the missions she hadn't known of, when Rex was sent to terminate a problematic Russian expat, and not only did so, but in the process implicated a child pornographer that hadn't even been on MI5's radar.

He also told her how Rex went to Naples and prevented a major arms deal between a terrorist group and the Camorra, the mafia group operating out of the Campania region in Italy with their headquarters in Naples.

Then, Josh speculated that if Rex had somehow hooked up with a well-trained military dog, the Saudi incident would be even more possible for him.

"You think it was a military dog, not a djinn?" Marissa asked, the scepticism clear in her tone.

Josh turned to stare at her in disbelief, then saw from her expression it was a rhetorical question. She was still talking.

"So, what do you want us to do, go hunting stories of evil spirits in the Saudi desert? If this was Rex, he's long gone. It's been months."

"Of course not," Brandt said, taking her question seriously, though she'd asked it with heavy sarcasm. "Look. Mutaib was a known arms smuggler and dealer. If it hadn't been for what I learned of his family life, so to speak, I'd think the raid was carried out by some official agency. The CIA, MI6, the Mossad. He was high on the hit lists of all of them. It could also have been one of his rival arms dealers. However, whispers are that the bastard had a few more wives in his harem than the authorities had on record. Those on record are all alive and well, still in the country, and now being taken care of by the Saudi government as is their right." He paused for breath, and Marissa jumped in.

"And?"

"And the ones not on record, but mentioned by the others, are the missing ones. And from what the Mabahith learned, all of them were foreigners who were there against their will. Naturally, the Saudi government doesn't want to know anything about these women—it could cause an international incident if the world learned that a member of the royal family had been participating in human trafficking."

Marissa made a derisive noise, and Brandt raised his eyebrows.

She said, "As if they weren't all…"

"Irrelevant," Brandt said firmly. "My point is that the household staff must know something. If nothing else, they know what the missing women looked like, and probably something about where they came from, maybe. I want you to go over there and talk to the staff, see if you can pick up a lead on the women, and then find and question them."

Brandt observed that both Josh and Marissa were looking uncertain. He went on. "I'll arrange matters so you won't be stopped. Trust me on that. See if you can find out who these women were, where they came from, maybe get pictures of them or use ID software to make sketches. Find out about that dog, and most important of all, show them Rex's picture and see if anyone recognizes him.

"You may as well be prepared to stay on this mission indefinitely, because you're looking for a needle in a haystack."

"And that's worth it to you, John?" Marissa made her voice tender as she asked.

Brandt ignored Josh as he captured Marissa's eyes with his. "You know it is. If he's dead, I can accept that. But if he's alive, I want to know why he hasn't reported in. Maybe he thinks we were involved in that ambush. I don't know the reason, but we don't leave our people behind, ever. I'd do the same for you, or Josh, or any of us. I need closure, Marissa."

Chapter Fifteen

When the sun rose in Phuket, Rex could see some of the devastation in the streets, but the news was of greater destruction to the west. Piecing it together, he realized his experience during the night was of the second or third wave. He couldn't account for why he'd been told that the tsunami was still on the way, when clearly it had hit the west coast before he'd even awakened.

Most of the beach communities due west of Phuket, including Sunstra's parents', were demolished. News reports were speaking in terms of survivors, not number of dead. The former number was much smaller, and the latter was so great that authorities weren't done counting. Speculation was that more bodies would be found far inland.

When he heard that, Rex knew he and Digger could help. Digger's nose and Rex's guidance could find some of them, and it would take all the trained search and rescue resources that could get there to avoid the worst of the consequences—disease from putrefying bodies of people and carcasses of animals.

It was going to be a massive effort.

He also felt he needed to stay in town to try to discover Sunstra's fate. He had to accept she was most likely dead, but if there were any chance she was alive, he wanted to know it.

Therefore, as soon as he'd fed Digger, Rex went to the nearest policeman and asked where he could volunteer his and his dog's services. He was directed to the central area where search and rescue efforts were being coordinated. There, he told the coordinators he was concerned about a friend, and he named the village where Sunstra's family had their home. From the look on their faces, he surmised there was very little hope Sunstra had survived. Nevertheless, he insisted to be assigned to that area.

"You must be prepared to find no survivors," they told him as diplomatically as they could. He smiled weakly and said he understood. He'd still like to search, and if it was okay, he'd return to the city when he or Digger needed a break, and search the survivor lists for his friend.

They gave him an orange vest for himself and one for Digger, indicating they were official searchers, and told him good luck.

Rex found a station where food was being issued to searchers and took enough for him and Digger for a day. He suspected Digger would need a break before he did. He'd heard snatches of conversation among the other searchers that their dogs were stressed when they found only dead bodies, as if they'd failed their mission to find their targets in time. The dogs needed lots of care and praise to avoid becoming depressed.

Anxious as he was to get started, he joined a queue to fill the gas tank of his rental car. Rather than sit in his car and wait for the line to move, he secured Digger's leash and let him out. Digger knew when he was on leash that he was working, or if not working, he wasn't free to explore unless Rex commanded him. He paced a bit, and then he sat down, looking around at the crowds and then up at Rex, as if to ask, "What's going on, mate?"

Rex, in turn, was searching the faces of the crowd. He'd be looking at faces until he found Sunstra, or word of her. If she'd gotten out in time, maybe she would've come here, knowing he'd be here looking for her? It was a long shot, not comforting at all.

The line crept forward slowly, and each time it moved a car length, Rex got in moved the car forward, then got out again and looked at the new people who joined the queue. It took nearly half an hour to get his turn at the pump. He didn't allow himself to get discouraged that he hadn't seen the face he was looking for. It would have been an almost impossible coincidence if he had.

When he'd filled the tank, he ordered Digger back into the car and resolutely headed for the beach. They'd search until Digger needed a break and repeat the process until the Thai authorities declared the search over, or until he found Sunstra or word of her. Worst case would be if her body was never found. He'd carry her image in his mind forever if that happened, wondering. If he'd been ready for a romance to blossom, would she have gone to visit her parents, or would she be safe in Bangkok right now?

Logically, he knew it wasn't his fault. Just like it wasn't his fault that his family had died at the hands of terrorists in that bombing in Spain. Emotionally, it was harder to process. The butterfly effect. If he'd been more serious about Sunstra, or if she'd never met him, would she be safe right now? Dodging the carcass of a goat near the place where the policeman had stopped him in the wee hours of the morning, Rex gave himself a mental shake.

Stop it! Torturing yourself with what ifs will do no one any good.

There was no barrier across the road now. Rex wondered if the officer had made it to safety. He shook his head and firmly turned his mind to the present. He and Digger had a grid to search, printed on a map the search coordinator had given him. They were to start at the edge of the water, search the beach and inland to where houses had been, walking back and forth for a quarter mile, every two feet until they reached the buildings. Then they must search any houses that remained standing, the rubble of those that had been destroyed, and in between. When that was done, if Digger wasn't too stressed, he'd take another section.

Digger would be the most valuable part of the team. If there was a body buried in shallow sand, or under the rubble of a house, Digger would alert to it. Rex's part was to flag anything he couldn't see without digging, and another crew, trained to clear the area, would take over. Naturally, if he found someone alive, he would alert the rescue crews and stay with the person until rescuers arrived.

Four hours after arriving at the coordinates he'd been given, Rex called a break. Digger had adjusted to the rhythms of the search. At first, he wanted to dig for everything they found, but after Rex shook his head at him for digging up a dead rooster, he seemed to understand he was just to alert, wait for Rex to plant the flags, and then keep moving.

From what Rex had seen so far, he hadn't expected to find any human remains. When he'd reached his area, there were no houses to be seen, and not much in the way of rubble. The tsunami had swept the beach as clean as if there'd never been a village there. In the first grid, he'd been correct, though there were a few animal carcasses. He suspected they'd been washed out as the first or second wave drew back, or maybe had been trapped in the collapsed houses that had also been swept out to sea.

After clearing his first grid, they were assigned to one further inland that had more buildings and trees. It was heartbreaking to find the bodies of entire families entangled in the remains of their homes. Impossible to tell what they might have been doing when the wave took their lives, but Rex suspected most had been asleep. They'd never had a chance. When he realized the extent of the damage, he couldn't escape the conclusion that Sunstra and her family had also perished. But he put it out of his mind and grimly searched on.

I have to see her just one more time, even if she is dead.

Digger was distressed after an hour of searching the second grid, so Rex had decided on a break, but he wouldn't leave the area until his entire assignment had been done. He led Digger back to their car and gave him a drink of water, then held and petted him until he stopped shaking. He reckoned it was a little too early to eat, and in fact he didn't feel like eating anything, himself. But Digger took a little kibble and some of the food Rex brought along. Rex hadn't thought to stuff the kong, but he got it out and tossed it to Digger anyway. The dog perked up and played for a while.

Rex had no idea how long a break he should give Digger before they started again, but when the dog picked up the kong in his mouth and brought it to him, he figured that was enough time. He took the toy, expecting a bit of resistance, but Digger let it go without protest and favored him with a happy smile. That convinced Rex they could finish the search.

"Hey buddy, I wish I could get a toy to play with that would unwind me like that kong unwinds you."

After another couple of hours, they were done with the second grid, the sun was setting, and Rex figured they were due a longer break. He urged Digger into the car and headed for Phuket. By the time they got there, it was late afternoon, and Rex hoped there'd be lists at the search coordinator's station with positive identification of at least some of the victims and survivors. He reckoned survivors would have made their way to Phuket, the nearest large city, in hopes of disaster relief. If Sunstra were among them, her name should be on a list. Maybe not today, or tomorrow, or… but he had already decided he'd stay until he got closure, one way or another.

As soon as he got within sight of the coordination site, he realized it wasn't going to be easy to see any such list. Hordes of people milled around the doorway, and he soon saw they were being ushered in just a few at a time.

"What do you think, boy? Should we join the crowd?"

Digger sat down and let out a long sigh, a sign he was content with whatever Rex decided.

Rex decided the sooner they got in line, the sooner they could get dinner somewhere, he could take a shower, and they could rest up for the next day. It was already too late in the day to continue the search, so he was confident every other searcher would be doing the same thing.

Dark was falling when he finally got into the building. The walls of the lobby were covered with paper, but when he got close enough to see, his heart sank. Every name was written in Thai script. His shoulders slumped. Speaking the language was one thing, he had no problem with that, but reading it was a totally different matter.

A soft voice interrupted his thoughts, and he recognized the accented English of a Thai speaker.

"Can I help you?"

Turning, he saw a diminutive woman with gray hair captured neatly in a bun at the nape of her neck. Her face was full of sympathy.

"Yes, ma'am. Thank you." Rex answered in English, then switched to Thai. "I seek the name of my friend. Sunstra Chevapravatgumrong."

"Come with me," she answered. She led him to a section a few feet away and began sweeping her hand down the list of names, repeating Sunstra's family name as she read. "Ah, here. Kraisee Chevapravatgumrong. He must be a relative."

"Crazy?" Rex repeated.

"Kraisee." She half smiled as she corrected his pronunciation, "It means lion, or brave as a lion."

Rex remembered Sunstra's explanation that family names were literally that.

No one can have a surname that isn't unique to their family. Is this her father? A brother?

Urgently, he asked, "Is this a list of survivors, or…"

"Yes," she answered. "Survivors. And here is where he can be reached." She gave an address, which Rex committed to memory.

"Thank you!" he exclaimed. It was the first time in eighteen hours when he thought there could be a glimmer of hope that she might be alive and with her family.

All thoughts of dinner and rest forgotten, he rushed out of the building. Digger kept pace with him, the leash limp, as they raced for the car. Rex impatiently tapped the address into his phone's GPS and learned the address was a residence.

Does that mean the relative, whoever it is, lives here or have they come here in time to escape the tsunami?

Rex didn't bother answering his own rhetorical questions as he drove to the address he was given, which turned out to be a few miles southeast of the city, situated on one of the low hills surrounding it.

When he reached the address, he told Digger to stay in the car. It was a modest home, only one story, but surrounded by neat gardens and looked to be a relatively recent construction. He approached the front door and pressed a button he assumed was the doorbell. Inside, a pleasant chime rang faintly. Rex stepped back and waited.

And waited.

A full two minutes passed before he reached to ring again and was startled by the door being snatched away from his hand. He let it fall to his side. He was facing a man a few years younger than him, who looked so much like Sunstra it could have been her, in drag. Except his face was unnaturally pale. Rex's mouth fell open.

"Yes? Do you bring word of my family?" the young man asked. He'd leaned forward on seeing Rex and was steadying himself with a hand on the door frame. "Please, are they safe?"

Rex found his voice. "I was hoping to ask you the same question. Are you Kraisee?"

To Rex's surprise, he found his shirt seized in both the young man's hands.

"Where is she?" he shouted.

"Whoa, hang on. Where is who?" Rex asked.

Behind him, Rex could hear Digger going nuts in the car, barking as if he'd treed a cat or a bad guy. Rex grabbed the man's wrists and squeezed until he let go of Rex's shirt. He kept hold of them as he said, "Let's start over. Are you Kraisee Chevapravatgumrong?"

Digger stopped barking.

"Yes, yes. Who wants to know?" After a slight struggle, Kraisee gave up trying to get out of Rex's grip, but on confirmation of who he was talking to, Rex let go.

"I'm Ruan Daniel. I have a friend, Sunstra Chevapravatgumrong. Is she your... sister?" Rex guessed.

"Where is she?" Kraisee shouted again.

At his shout, Digger started barking again.

"Look, I think we'd better settle down, before my dog breaks through the car window. Can we go inside and talk rationally? I'm looking for your sister, too. Let's compare notes. May I come in, and may I bring my dog?"

Kraisee looked beyond Rex toward the car and his expression grew doubtful. Rex assured him the dog wouldn't attack, so long as he kept his cool. Kraisee nodded.

Rex went to the car and let Digger out but kept him on leash. Something was wrong here, and Rex wanted to get to the bottom of it.

Kraisee waited at the door, and when Rex and Digger approached, he stood aside and swept his hand inward in a gesture of welcome.

"I'm sorry," he said, in English as good as his sister's. "I have been mad with worry since we got the demand."

It was Rex's turn to be confused. "Demand?"

"The ransom demand."

Now Rex was doubly confused, thunderstruck. "Wait— you're not worried about her because of the tsunami?"

"Oh, my God, I hadn't thought about that! What if they were holding her in the danger zone?" Kraisee, who had gestured for Rex to sit and had taken a seat himself, jumped up again, agitated and tearing at his hair.

Digger growled.

"Kraisee, please calm yourself. You're making my dog nervous, and trust me, you don't want to do that. Start at the beginning and tell me what you're talking about."

Rex's composed yet firm tone seemed to calm the young man. He flopped down into the chair again, and Digger relaxed.

"To answer your questions, yes, Sunstra is my sister. My younger sister," he clarified. "Two days ago, she disappeared. We thought at first her friend had come early. Wait —are you the friend who was planning to visit on Friday?"

Rex nodded. "Today, yes. But the tsunami…"

"Of course, yes. I've been so worried about Sunstra that I barely gave attention to the tsunami."

Rex thought that was an extraordinary statement, but he let it go. "So Sunstra went missing before the tsunami?" he asked, to make sure he'd heard Kraisee correctly.

"Yes, yes. On Wednesday. She went to Phuket to shop, and she didn't come home. We were worried only a little, but my mother said she must have met you early."

Rex opened his mouth to speak, but Kraisee rushed on.

"She didn't, we know that now. On Thursday, we got the demand. My parents must sign over their land, or Sunstra would be harmed."

Chapter Sixteen

Rex felt a little less confused, and a lot more hopeful about Sunstra's survival. Now he had to convince Kraisee to explain what the demand was all about and to let him help search for Sunstra. But first, what had happened to her parents?

"Kraisee, I know you don't know me, but I'm going to ask you to trust me when I say I can help you. Sunstra has become a dear friend and very important to me in the short time I've known her. So believe me, her safety is my highest priority. Is this about some family business? What land are we talking about here, and why do the kidnappers want it?"

Kraisee gasped again. "Kidnappers!"

Rex smiled gently. "Yes, that's what we call those who capture and hold people illegally and against their will. What do you call them?"

Kraisee nodded, his mouth twisted in fear and revulsion. "I know what a kidnapper is, but in this case, we call them politicians. I'm sorry, let me begin from the beginning, and if you can help, I'll gladly accept it."

"That sounds like a good plan." To Digger, Rex gestured with his hand to relax.

When the dog was settled on his belly, with his forelegs balancing him and his head up, his eyes alertly and intelligently fixed on Kraisee, the young man took a deep breath and began at what he considered the beginning—the land.

"My parents are not wealthy. My father worked a part-time job to pay his way through medical school and became a doctor. After he qualified, he returned to his home village in the Mueang Phan district, in the Lampang province up north, close to the border of Myanmar, where he set up his practice. He did all right, and we were given the opportunities to study after school, succeed in business, and have a few luxuries, but great wealth, no.

"Our family's land is near the village, but my father chose not to farm it. It has lain fallow for forty years or more. A few years ago, the largest zinc deposit in Thailand was found nearby. It is a rich deposit of valuable mineral, but the mining is a blight on the landscape!"

Rex didn't want to upset Kraisee, but this was going too slowly. "What does that have to do with your family's land?"

"Oh," said Kraisee, blinking. "Didn't I say? Our land has the same Jurassic strata as the zinc mine. Over the years, various corrupt politicians have been trying to take it away from my father. My father does not want it mined, so he will not sell it."

Rex sat back in his chair. So *that* was the motive. "What's the rest of the story?" he urged.

"My father is well-known and well-liked by the people of his village, including some who have worked their way up in the government. Until recently, the attempts to steal our land have been blocked by those friends. But in the past few months, efforts have intensified. We—my parents, my older brother, Sunstra, and myself—gathered at my parent's vacation home on the beach to discuss what to do. And then Sunstra didn't come home on Thursday night, as I said."

"I take it this is your home. Where are your parents and older brother?"

"No, this is my brother's home. He is also a physician, and he has done well for himself. He asked me to stay here and look after our business in town while he accompanied my parents to Pha Daeng."

Rex curbed his impatience. Kraisee was obviously in shock and highly distressed over Sunstra's fate, but his disjointed telling of the story was frustrating.

Where the heck is Pha Daeng? Are they safe? Why did they go there?

Rather than pepper the man with his questions, Rex cut to the chase with some assumptions.

"Your parents and older brother are on their way to sign over the land for Sunstra's safe return, is that right?"

"Yes," Kraisee answered. "To us, nothing is as valuable as my sister's life."

"Agreed. And I take it the land is not in the tsunami area?"

"Oh, no! It is far to the north. Almost to the border with Myanmar."

"Okay. So, can you get in touch with them? Maybe they don't want to be so hasty to comply with the demands."

Kraisee stared at Rex, a frown marring his smooth forehead and his mouth slightly open. After a few seconds, he exclaimed, "Of course they will comply with the demands! How else can we guarantee my sister's safety? Are you insane?"

Rex took a deep breath. He was about to put a scare into Kraisee, but he was certain he had more experience with this type of crisis than the young man or his family.

"You can't guarantee her safety by complying. The most dangerous time for the perpetrators in this type of kidnapping is when they have to deliver on their promise, in other words, when they have to return their captive after getting what they want. Keep in mind, she now knows who they are, she may have seen their faces. How will they keep their illegal actions quiet if they let her go? Once they have what they want, there is no motivation to keep her alive."

Rex hadn't thought it possible for Kraisee to turn any paler, but his face turned a few lighter shades of gray as Rex spoke.

"Then it is hopeless!" he cried.

"No, not at all, but you'll have to listen to me, and do as I tell you."

"What do you... what experience..."

Rex held his hand up to stop him, "Kraisee, we don't have time for that. You'll have to trust that I know what I'm doing. Now, just contact your parents and tell them to stall. Demand proof of life. That's the first step. We want a picture, or better yet, a video, of Sunstra, unharmed, holding the latest newspaper with the date showing prominently. She should be allowed to speak and tell us she's okay.

"I want to see the video, so I can determine whether she's been given a script. Meanwhile, I'll get some help figuring out where she was on Thursday before the abduction. Pull yourself together, Kraisee—we need to move fast."

Kraisee nodded. "All right, I'll do it. But my parents may want to speak to you and learn what you know about kidnappings. Why you are so confident that stalling is the best course of action now."

"I'll speak to them if that's what they want. Do you mind if we, my dog and I, stay here? It will be easier to coordinate our efforts if we're in the same place."

"Certainly! My brother would never forgive me for not extending our hospitality to a friend of Sunstra's. Are you hungry or thirsty?"

"Let's put things in motion and then come back to that question. Digger and I have had dinner. We don't need anything right now."

Digger had laid his chin on his front paws as the conversation went on, but his ears showed he was alert and listening. Every time Sunstra's name was mentioned, they swiveled toward the speaker. He alerted to the word 'dinner' as well, which made Kraisee laugh despite his tension.

"Digger, is that your dog's name?"

"Yes."

"Curious name. It looks like he would like more dinner, if you ask me."

Rex smiled. "That's okay, he always acts as if he's being starved to death. He'll wait. Now call your parents."

Before leaving India, Rex had set up Rehka, the woman he'd originally gone to Saudi Arabia to rescue, as his financial administrator and IT support person. Part of her job was to help hack into the hard drives he'd 'liberated' in his raid on Usama, an Afghani drug lord's, compound. He was certain there'd be information on where Usama had stored his vast wealth, and since the man had no more use for it, being dead, Rex reckoned he was entitled to spoils of war. He was still working on a plan to get some of the money he hoped to extract to the families of the men in his team who were killed. It was not as if he could just mail them a check with a note saying, hey, I'm Rex Dalton, and I was there when your loved one was killed, but I survived and here is some money for you.

The Saudi rescue operation turned out to be much bigger than just Rehka Gyan, and he thought it was fortunate that Rehka had just the skills he needed, having been trained as an accountant and IT specialist before falling into the debt that landed her in a human trafficking situation. He'd taken her and six of her fellow 'pleasure wives' from the monster, Mutaib, who'd bought them as sex slaves. In the process of ridding the world of Mutaib, he'd also liberated valuables and computers from him, and he'd given Rehka the task of tracking down the money in offshore accounts, extracting it and putting it in a trust, as well as administering it for her benefit and that of the other women.

Anticipating the need to communicate with her privately from time to time, Rex had also asked Rehka to set up an unbreakable secure system for them to speak to each other in real time. She'd come through with flying colors. It was Rehka he intended to contact now about finding Sunstra's financial tracks, Finint as it was referred to in the intelligence community, for the day she'd disappeared.

Rex figured CRC's own security experts couldn't have done a better job than Rehka had. She had equipped them both with encrypted satellite phones. Rex's phone was encased in a shockproof and waterproof casing, because he would be out and about in nature and some rough places with his phone. Hers was daintier and looked like a normal mobile phone.

The phones' ringers were set to sound like a normal smartphone. On close inspection of the two phones, however, it was evident that the phones were programmed with only the other phone's number. Rehka had only Rex's number on her phone, and Rex had only Rehka's number on his.

If someone were really, really technical, understood the latest and greatest in secure communications and encryptions, and had a lot of time, he might have been able to figure out that every call made through these phones were end-to-end protected. Each phone had an encryption app, developed by Rehka, running on it. Each app had encryption keys, and they expected and accepted only keys from the app on the other phone. In other words, it was impossible for a man-in-the-middle attack to be successful.

Apart from the encryption, the signals from the phones were digitized and sent over the internet through a heavily encrypted virtual private network tunnel, which was routed and rerouted through no less than twelve virtual telephone switches located across the globe. Only after a worldwide tour through a maze of virtual telephone-switch destinations did the signal arrive at the sender's or receiver's phone, though the trip took less than a second.

It was not impossible to tap into their conversations, but to do it, someone would need one of the phones in his hand, he'd need the password to unlock the phone, and he'd need to know the passphrases, which Rex and Rehka had agreed on beforehand. He'd have to give that passphrase to the other party when they made the connection and before they would say anything. The passphrases were set up to sound like a normal greeting between two normal people about to have a normal conversation, but certain words in the phrases would signal if the other party was under duress or not. That is, any mention of weather meant things were okay. No mention of the weather meant things were not okay.

Rex went out to the car and retrieved his luggage, Digger's bowls and kibble, and of course, the kong. Digger was too well-behaved to jump at the toy, but he gave his happy smile and wagged his tail excitedly when he saw it.

"Sorry, buddy. We don't have time to play right now, but I'll make it up to you as soon as I can." Rex lugged everything into the house and headed in the direction of the room Kraisee had indicated before he called his parents.

The young man was still on the phone with them, listening and then answering in rapid Thai, when Rex passed him. Rex paused and lifted an eyebrow. Kraisee nodded and gave Rex a thumbs-up, which startled him at first. He'd learned from Sunstra that only children used that gesture, and it meant something far less positive than its international meaning—more or less the equivalent of an upraised middle finger. But when Rex glanced at Kraisee's face in confusion, he saw a smile and a nod that told him Kraisee had meant it the American way—everything was okay. He returned it, smiled, nodded, and continued to his room.

Once there, he dug through his effects until he found what he was looking for, the satellite phone. Through a curious anomaly in time zones, Phuket was only an hour and a half ahead of Mumbai time, and although it was nearly midnight in Phuket, the time was not alarmingly late in Mumbai—not quite ten p.m. Too late for a social call, to be sure, but not so late that Rehka would be startled out of sleep.

Rex dialed and waited.

When the passphrases had been exchanged, Rex's mentioning the tsunami though it wasn't strictly speaking a weather event, Rehka was more than intelligent enough to understand Rex was okay. He asked how she was doing and if he'd awakened her.

"Oh, my goodness, no, Ruan. I have just returned from seeing a film with Vidya Patel. Aarav was kind enough to do the babysitting which allowed us to have a nice girl's night. How can I help you?" Her tone was light, unstressed.

It pleased Rex that she was doing so well after the ordeal in Saudi Arabia. She was a strong woman.

With her in such good spirits, he didn't want to burst her bubble, but there was no easy way he could tell her what he wanted and why, without her remembering her own situation just a few months ago. "Rehka, I need your help on an urgent matter. It isn't for me, but for a friend. I'm afraid she's been kidnapped, and her captors have a two-day head start on us."

Rehka's tone conveyed she'd grasped the seriousness of the situation immediately, but it was also clear it had brought up memories she was trying to forget. She was quiet for a long while, Rex didn't speak. He knew she needed the time to compose herself. Then she cleared her throat and said, "What can I do to help, Ruan?"

"Can you hack her credit cards and bank account? We need a location of her last known whereabouts."

"I can. Just give me her card number or bank account details," she said without hesitation.

Rex gave Sunstra's name and spelled out the impossible surname, and the bank account details, which Kraisee provided. Rehka read everything back to him to be certain she had it correct. Then she said, "Give me some time. I'll be in touch when I have it."

"Can you do it tonight? It's a matter of life and death."

"Ruan, since you say it is a matter of life and death, I will do it yesterday." The lilt at the end of the sentence let him know she was smiling. Then she grew more serious. "Ruan...is it... ah... a situation like mine and the others? The pleasure wives?"

"No. She's being held for ransom. Unfortunately, there's no time to explain. Please, get that information to me as soon as possible. I can't do anything until I know where she was two days ago, on Thursday, when she was abducted."

"I'll get on it right now."

With nothing to do but wait, Rex returned to find Kraisee. The young man was off the phone by the time Rex located him in the kitchen. Digger had been shadowing Rex, as usual, and the dog had evidently decided Kraisee was a friend. He walked up to the young man and leaned against his leg. Rex thought it might have had more to do with the fact that Kraisee was scrambling some eggs than genuine friendship and concern for the young man.

Kraisee had guessed right—scrambled eggs were a particular treat for Digger. Rex thought too late about the kong and Digger's bowl. Kraisee was already bending down with a plate of eggs to place it in front of the dog. Digger's tail wagged rapidly as he practically inhaled them.

"How did you know?" Rex asked, smiling.

"We always had dogs at home," Kraisee answered, his gaze on Digger. "I miss owning a pet. Digger is very smart, isn't he?"

Rex had told Sunstra that Digger was his emotional support dog, so he didn't hesitate to tell Kraisee that the dog was not only smart, but well-trained. He mentioned their day of search and rescue.

Kraisee's hand went to his forehead. "I'm so sorry... I keep forgetting the tragedy that has struck my country. I can only think of Sunstra. Did you find... Are there many dead?"

"I don't have a count," Rex answered. "But on a positive note, I can say there are entire walls of survivor names. We can only hope the death toll is much smaller. I found your name that way," he continued.

"Really? How curious. I did not report my whereabouts to authorities."

Rex stared at him. That was curious indeed, and it might be important. "Excuse me, I need to make another call."

He returned to his room and went through the ritual to call Rehka again.

"I don't have anything, yet, Ruan. I will call you when I do."

"I understand. But I've just discovered something that may be important. I don't know if you can do it, but after you get Sunstra's movements on Thursday, can you see if there were many calls to the rescue coordinators' headquarters earlier today? Someone reported her brother as a survivor, and it wasn't him. We don't know the motive, or who it could have been, but if there's a chance the kidnappers are keeping tabs on her family, one of the calls could have been from them."

"That's what Americans call a long shot, isn't it, Ruan?"

"Yep. But sometimes long shots hit home. Sunstra's movements first, then a list of the phone numbers calling this one." He recited the number of the rescue headquarters. Chances were there'd be hundreds, but even a large amount of data could be quickly checked against other databases. If he had the full resources of CRC behind him, it wouldn't even take very long. It might take Rehka longer, however with him guiding her efforts, it was doable.

After securing Rehka's cooperation, Rex hung up again, for the first time noticing Digger hadn't followed him back to the room. He found the dog enjoying pets and scratches from Kraisee, a blissful look on both faces.

Hmmm. Maybe Digger's a great emotional support dog after all.

Chapter Seventeen

Rex suggested that Kraisee should probably get some rest, it was obvious he'd been awake and stressed far too long. He admitted he hadn't slept since late Thursday night, and it was already forty-eight hours since then. The man was practically out on his feet.

Kraisee answered that he'd try, but he didn't have much hope of sleeping. As he left the room, he mentioned that although his parents had agreed to stall, his older brother, Narong, was on his way to Phuket on the first flight he could get. Narong wasn't happy with the plan but agreed to talk to Rex face-to-face before making a final decision.

"He'll be here first thing in the morning. Maybe you should get some rest yourself," Kraisee concluded.

"I'm waiting for some information, but you're right. We should all be fresh for whatever tomorrow brings. I'll turn in as soon as I hear back from my contact."

Without further question, Kraisee continued toward his room, while Rex returned to his. This time, Digger went with him. Rex thought about ordering the dog to stay with

Kraisee, but he decided maybe exhaustion would help the other man to sleep, while he needed some distraction to keep him awake. Besides, he'd promised Digger a kong session.

Rex looked over the room carefully to make sure there was nothing Digger could break if he bumped into the furniture in his enthusiasm for the kong. The furnishings were simple yet appeared of high quality. Décor was sparse, and he found nothing that would be in danger.

Speaking quietly, he settled Digger before giving him the kong. Instead of tossing it to set it bouncing and excite Digger too much, he handed it to the dog, who took it gently in his mouth. Digger seemed to understand it was late, and he didn't need to go crazy. Instead, he lay down on his belly with the toy and began to gnaw it like a bone. That was good enough for Rex. Digger never ceased to amaze him with his spot-on understanding of situations.

He kept up a running conversation with his mute buddy while he waited for Rehka's call, but Digger was too busy with the kong to respond to anything. So, the soliloquy quickly wore him down and he lost the struggle against his heavy eyelids. The day's and previous nights' events had worn him out, and tonight's revelation about Sunstra's danger hadn't helped.

He wasn't sure for how long he'd slept when the sat-phone's ringing woke him. He was so impatient for the information that the elaborate security dance, though it took only seconds, irritated him.

"Rehka, finally!" he said. He instantly regretted his abrupt words. "I'm sorry. I'm sure you did everything as quickly as possible."

"It's all right. You must be under a great deal of stress. This woman is special to you?"

Rex was quick to answer. "Just friends, but a special friend, yes. Like you."

Her voice sounded as if she might be smiling again when she answered. "Okay, then let's waste no more time. Your friend did some clothes shopping, had lunch at an inexpensive restaurant, bought theater tickets, and finally visited a jewelry store, where she bought two watches, a woman's and a man's."

Hmmm.

When Rex made no further comment, Rehka went on. "The last visit was fortunate. There is security video footage, and I was able to download it. She is very beautiful, Ruan."

"Yeah, I only befriend beautiful ladies, like yourself," Rex flattered her, then started laughing and was relieved to hear a giggle from the other end. "Was there anyone else with her in the store?"

"Not when she walked in, but a man came in after she had been there for a few minutes. It seemed he was trying to avoid the camera, but I was able to get two images, one full-face and one in profile. I isolated the still shots, and I can send them to you if you want."

"Do you have any reason to believe he's related to the kidnapping?"

"Nothing directly, but as I said, he was obviously trying to avoid the camera. And then, when she left, he followed without engaging the clerk."

"That sounds suspicious, all right. Would you send me the addresses of everywhere she went, as well as those two pictures? And can you get a still of Sunstra? They probably have pictures of her here, but just in case, so I can show them to the store employees?"

"Of course. Anything else?"

"Those calls to…"

"Oh, yes," she interrupted. "I have that list. It's a lot of calls, Ruan."

"I understand. What databases could you hack to try to identify who the numbers belong to? Can we get names, maybe even addresses?"

"I think so, but I need some rest, so I don't do anything to alert the data providers that I'm in their systems. They have defensive mechanisms to shut down intrusions, and then we wouldn't be able to finish the job."

"I understand. Get some rest, and then that's top priority for tomorrow, okay?"

"First thing. Got it."

Now we're getting somewhere.

Nothing more could be done that night, even after Rex had downloaded the encrypted email with the images and the list of phone numbers. He looked at the image of the mysterious man who'd evidently been following Sunstra. Maybe Kraisee could identify him, or maybe he was just a hired thug. Kraisee needed his rest, so it could wait until morning.

The list of numbers wouldn't be of any use until they had names to go with them. There were far too many to begin dialing them and asking if the person answering had kidnapped anyone lately.

Rex looked at the file with Sunstra's image last. She looked happy, and more beautiful than he even remembered. Who was the man's watch for? Her father? One of her brothers? He'd have to remember to ask Kraisee in the morning if any of them had a birthday coming up.

Just before he drifted off to sleep, Digger's weight made the bed dip. "Digger, off," he mumbled before sleep took him.

As he dreamed that night, disturbing images of

Sunstra's drowned visage kept him restless. He felt a weight on his chest and his subconscious mind interpreted it as great grief and a sense of having just missed something very important to him.

Digger remained vigilant. His human friend was distressed, but Digger could detect no imminent danger. So, he did the only thing he could. He laid his big head on Rex's chest and joined him in sleep.

————

Despite the length and anxieties of the previous day, Rex woke refreshed and relieved to see the cause of his heavy chest.

"Digger," he groaned, "I told you to get off."

Digger's nose was pointed at Rex's chin, and when he heard Rex's voice, he lazily opened the eye that wasn't buried in Rex's chest. Rex had lifted his head just enough to see the dog's face. "Yes, I'm talking to you, mutt."

He couldn't keep the amusement and affection out of his voice. Digger's tail thumped once, painfully, against Rex's bare calf.

"Okay, not kidding now. Off. I need to get up."

Digger bounded to his feet, still on the bed, and then dropped lightly off to the floor. He went to the door and looked back and forth between it and Rex, clearly indicating he needed to be let out for his morning constitutional.

"Give me a minute," Rex said. He knew if push came to shove, the dog could open the door himself, but he wouldn't unless he was told to do so. A few moments later, he had a pair of pants and t-shirt on and was leading Digger outside when a male voice he didn't recognize, raised in anger, arrested his attention and his progress.

"How do you know who this man is? Did Sunstra ever show us his picture? No! She did not! For all we know, *he* is the kidnapper!"

Rex surmised quickly that the voice belonged to Narong, and that the recipient of the scolding was the younger of the brothers, Kraisee. With a hand gesture, Rex commanded Digger to wait where he was, while he stepped into the room to support Kraisee.

"Hold up, there, cowboy," he said. "If you've got a beef with me, take it up with me."

Both men turned to him, and they bore identical expressions. Rex figured Kraisee's meant, "Are you out of your mind?" and Narong's meant, "Who the hell are you?"

He repeated his hand gesture, so Digger wouldn't get into the act, and let himself smile. "No offense. I assure you, I haven't kidnapped your sister. I'm her friend, and I'm as anxious as you to see her returned safely to her family."

Narong had collected himself by that time, though Kraisee still looked as if he thought Rex had picked up a live grenade. The older brother stepped forward aggressively. "What proof do you have?"

"Difficult to prove a negative, but if you meant proof that I'm her friend, would a picture of your sister playing with my dog settle it?"

Narong raised his eyebrows without answering, and Rex took it as assent. He reached inside his pocket for his cell phone and pulled it out. Narong relaxed slightly but crossed his arms over his chest.

Didn't Kraisee tell me his brother was a doctor? Why is he built like a Navy SEAL? And acting like a bear with a sore tooth?

Rex found a picture of Sunstra, her hair blown back in the wind, a look of pure joy on her face, hugging Digger. He handed the phone to Narong with his left hand, while signaling Digger to come with his right. A moment later, he felt Digger's solid presence at his side, as Narong studied the picture and then the dog.

Narong handed the phone back to Rex. "My apologies. My sister's abduction has put us all on edge."

"No worries. I'm a little touchy myself. My dog needs to go outside. Can we take this up in a few minutes? I have news."

"Certainly. Kraisee, would you mind preparing breakfast for our guest?"

Half an hour later, Rex and Digger were both on cloud nine from the amazing breakfast Kraisee had prepared. It hadn't occurred to Rex to ask him what his occupation was, but during the interval before Kraisee announced it was ready, Narong had filled him in. Kraisee was a chef at one of the posh hotels in Phuket. After breakfast, Rex would have sworn on a stack of Bibles that Kraisee was *the* top chef in Thailand, not just Phuket.

In the same interval, he'd rapidly told Narong what Rehka had found and had learned in turn that the reason Narong was built like a Navy SEAL was that he'd been one, in the Thai navy. His medical training had come first, and then he'd enlisted and was part of a team that was regularly assigned to search and rescue, which often required emergency medical care for the rescued even before they were taken to hospitals. Only five years after leaving the Navy, his practice in Phuket was booming.

However, he wasn't entirely convinced that Rex had the right approach, which was to play for time while making a plan to set her free.

"Listen, I appreciate your willingness to help, but you don't know Thailand. We must co-exist with this type of corruption, and it doesn't surprise us at all. You don't need to worry about Sunstra. Losing our land is maddening, but it is not as important as Sunstra's safety. My father will sign it over, Sunstra will be returned safely, and next week my father will be invited to dine with the district administrator, who is one of the men forcing the sale, and everything will be fine. No, we won't forgive or forget. But we won't fight it, either. There is no point."

Before Rex could respond, Narong went on. "However, if the bargain isn't kept, and she is hurt in any way, I'm going to war against them, and nothing will stop me."

That changed Rex's direction when he responded. "Why wait and see if they hurt her or not, Narong? I think you should prevent it not wait for it to happen. In any event, you may have been the medic on a Thai SEAL team, but you're going to get your sister killed and yourself in serious trouble if you retaliate as a one-man army. Let me help you."

Narong's expression went from annoyed to frankly irritated. "Excuse me. I am trying to be polite to you, a guest in my home. However, my brother has told me why you have a dog. I doubt that a man who has need of a service dog will be of any help."

Rex smiled. Since the events that sent him underground, he'd never felt the need to explain his former profession and he was not about to change that. So, his answer was a cryptic, "You'd be surprised." He had a fleeting thought about giving Sunstra's brothers a demonstration of what his 'service dog' was actually trained to do but quickly decided against it.

Narong paused a beat and intently looked Rex up and down, apparently in the process also noticing Rex's hair, currently in need of a haircut as well as being tousled from sleep and the lack of a morning shower yet.

"You don't look like you're in the military."

Rex said, "That's because I'm not."

"You don't look like you're in the police either."

"That's because I'm not," Rex answered.

Narong said, "So, not in the military, not in the police—then you must be a tourist."

"That I am." Rex smiled broadly.

Narong shook his head and gave an exaggerated sigh. "This is serious stuff. You could get hurt, maybe even killed. You and your dog."

All Rex needed was a base of operations and for the Chevapravatgumrong family to stall. If the brothers weren't going to be of any help, he would do it on his own. He had always operated better on his own, and lately, with Digger as his companion, he was even more lethal than ever before. He wasn't going to show his hand. They could play their cards. He would act accordingly.

He shrugged. "Well, my travel agent promised me an adventure holiday in Thailand, and so far, I've seen very little adventure. I'll take my chances."

"Okay, have it your way, don't blame me if you get injured or killed, and make sure you don't get in my way."

Rex nodded. "I promise." He looked at Digger, who was sitting there looking at them with a big smile, enjoying the repartee if Rex had to guess.

"You hear that Digger? We're not to get in this guy's way. It might get dangerous. You okay with that?"

Digger woofed.

"Kraisee, thanks for breakfast. It was outstanding. Narong, would you prefer I move into a hotel?"

"Please, that will not be necessary. A friend of Sunstra's is always welcome in my home."

"In that case, could you let me hook into your home network? I have a few pages of data to print."

"Certainly." Narong set Rex up in his own office, gave him the WiFi password, and reluctantly agreed with Rex to talk to his father and convince him to bring up the proof of life issue before signing over the land for the ridiculous price of one-thousand bhat, which the kidnappers had insisted upon paying so that the contract would look legal.

Rex began printing the list Rehka had sent that morning, which now included names in Thai and a column that transliterated those names so that Rex could attempt to pronounce them. She had cross-referenced them with various government databases, so that anyone who worked for the government in any capacity was identified with columns for the names of their agencies and their titles within the agency.

Rex was printing only that subset of the numbers, a list that required about ten pages. Narong came back in before the last page had finished printing and reported that his father would cooperate.

"What do you have there?" he asked.

Rex explained what he had and why he'd asked for it but looked out the window without answering when Narong asked how he'd gotten it. Fortunately, Narong was so distracted by his sister's dilemma and impressed with Rex's reasoning regarding the list that he didn't insist on an answer. How he got the list was not important. The fact that he had it was.

"That's very clever," he said. "Let me look at it. I can identify the names of individuals I know, and of those known to be corrupt even if I don't know them personally. That will narrow the search, yes?"

"Exactly what I was thinking, Narong. Once you've

narrowed it down, we can go to work on the crooked ones, maybe get a clue. See, we can work together after all. But I'll be sure not to get in your way if it comes to a fight."

"Excellent idea. How did you come up with it?"

"When Kraisee said he hadn't reported himself as safe to the emergency center, I started wondering who did, and why. Whoever did it was keeping tabs on your family, and reporting Kraisee as a survivor was an improvised message to a conspirator. In other words, 'Kraisee is still in town. Be careful.'"

Narong still looked confused. "Why couldn't they just make a call?"

"My guess is one or more of the kidnappers was in the danger zone when the tsunami hit. There could be any number of reasons this message needed to be conveyed in this way, but the simplest of them is that somehow their communications lines were cut, either literally or because one of them went missing. Maybe it's a blind chain. What's clear to me is there's something more valuable than zinc on your land, and the stakes are higher for the kidnappers than we knew."

Narong turned pale like his brother had the night before. "Which means it's even more dangerous for Sunstra!"

"Now you're getting the picture. So, let's get that list narrowed down, and then we can go rattle some cages. We also need to take these pictures to that jewelry store and see what the clerk can tell us."

Chapter Eighteen

The jewelry store clerk was arrogant and unhelpful and got Rex into a bad mood when he made shooing motions at Digger. He shook his head at the pictures of the man who'd followed Sunstra in and claimed he'd never seen the man, though he did remember Sunstra and her purchase. He smirked as he looked from Narong to Rex, as if he thought they were rivals for the girl's affection and wanted to know who the man's watch was for. Rex had the impulse to wipe the smirk off the clerk's face but decided a dust-up wouldn't make any difference except to his ego. He let it go.

They quickly went to the other places Sunstra had been as evidenced by her credit card and bank records, but since the jewelry store was the last chronologically, they didn't expect any help, and that proved to be true. A few remembered her, but none saw her follower.

Narong was discouraged as they went back to the house. Kraisee had prepared a nice lunch, but he informed them that the restaurant where he worked would be open soon, so he had to leave.

Narong gave a dispirited wave, saying, "That's all right. You can't help, anyway."

Rex caught the hurt look Kraisee turned on his brother, but Narong had his head in his hands and didn't see it. When Kraisee left the house, Rex started talking about his younger brother. He hadn't said a word about him to anyone since he broke up with the woman who would have been his wife if his family hadn't been killed.

"I had a younger brother once. They can be a pain in the rear, I know."

Narong lifted his head and stared at Rex. "What?"

"The way you spoke to Kraisee. Dismissing him. He must be a screw-up and a disappointment, right? Just being a chef and all, instead of a doctor."

Narong puffed up like a bantam rooster. "How dare you! Kraisee is a great chef. Someday, he'll own a chain of fine restaurants. You barely know him, or me. Why would you assume..." He broke off, noticing Rex's smile. "Wait, you said you *once* had. What..."

Rex took a deep breath. This was going to be difficult, but he had to do it to make his point.

"My brother was killed, along with my sister and my parents, in a terrorist explosion in Spain a few years back. I miss them every day. And I'd like to take back every careless word I said that might have made him feel he wasn't worthy. What you said—that Kraisee couldn't help—it hurt him."

Narong's face fell. "I didn't mean..."

"I know you didn't. I'm just saying, sometimes you have to lose something before you realize how much it meant to you. I reckon at times like these, family should support each other and must be extra sensitive about each other. If you lose Sunstra..."

Narong was instantly furious. "We *will* not lose her

unless your reckless scheme backfires! Leave my relationship with my brother out of this."

Rex nodded and excused himself. Digger needed a run, and his play to get Narong riled up instead of despairing had worked. Maybe it would also help Narong to acknowledge his rudeness and change the dynamic he had with his brother. That would be a good thing. He only felt a little bad about using the ploy to achieve his own ends.

A partner paralyzed by despair is worse than no partner at all.

When he got back into the house, Narong was deep in study of the list of people who'd called the rescue coordination center's phone number. As soon as he finished and narrowed the list to politicians and others who might have an interest in the Chevapravatgumrong land, they'd start visiting each one to question them and assess who might know something.

As Rehka had said, it was a long shot. Maybe one of the people whose name Narong didn't know was responsible, but they had to start somewhere. Rex knew it to be what policemen dreaded most, the painstaking attention to detail that turned up a clue, which led to another and another. Only they had a limited amount of time before their stall tactics backfired. For now, the ball was in the court of the kidnappers to supply proof of life, but once they'd done that the clock would start ticking again.

Out of the more than one hundred names on the list, Narong knew about half slightly, but only a dozen or so did he know to be corrupt or in a position to benefit from his family's land. The most expedient way of questioning them all was to start with the one whose home or place of business was nearest. That happened to be a minor bureaucrat within the Natural Resources department who lived nearby.

Half an hour later, they left the bureaucrat's home with

Narong second-guessing the strategy. "I have made an enemy that I didn't have before. It will have consequences."

"You can apologize later, Narong. What's important now is Sunstra. We're running out of time. Who on your list is someone who has tried before to get your father to sell, even if it seemed friendly?"

Narong read over his short-list and pointed to one name. "I know this man has bothered my father before. He is the undersecretary of mining and development in the Natural Resources department."

"Then let's go talk to him."

Fortunately, the man they were going to visit lived a short distance from where they started. Narong thought he might be in his office, though, which was in downtown Phuket. That turned out to be the case when they found only his wife and a servant at his home. They took polite leave of the wife without giving their names or indicating that they had some urgent matter to discuss with her husband. They left her with the message that it was nothing important, and they would phone his office and set up a meeting for later in the week.

Arriving at the undersecretary's office, at first, their errand was impeded by an administrative assistant who told them firmly the undersecretary could not be disturbed if they didn't have an appointment. It took only five-hundred bhat to 'remind' the assistant that they did indeed have an appointment.

The undersecretary sprang from his chair when they were ushered in. Another two-hundred and fifty bhat had ensured that the assistant wouldn't remind the undersecretary of their appointment. After all, it was on his calendar, no?

While the assistant scurried back to his desk to make

sure the appointment showed up when the undersecretary looked later, Narong and Rex were advancing on the man in a threatening manner.

Rex signaled Digger to be quiet, though. He didn't want the dog's presence to become an issue before it was really necessary, and besides, he'd promised Narong not to get in his way if it came to a fight. He allowed Narong to gain a step on him and take the lead in the questioning.

Narong wasted no time in going on the offensive. "Where is my sister?" he demanded.

Rex observed the undersecretary's body language and expressions as he carefully arranged his face to appear surprised.

"Why, I don't know what you're talking about!" he exclaimed. "Why would I know *who* your sister is, not to mention where she is. Who are you, anyway?"

Narong's fists were clenched as he took another step forward, getting right in the undersecretary's face. "Mee Noi, you know very well who I am. You know my family, and you definitely know my sister. I'm only going to ask you one more time. What interest do you have in my father's land, and what have you done with my sister?"

Mee Noi, whose name meant Little Bear, which at this stage, might as well have meant 'Little Shaky', took a step back and tried to bluff an answer again. "Oh, Narong! Now I recognize you. But I still don't know what you mean. What's this about your father's land? And your sister?"

Narong's patience, not long in the first place, was exhausted. He drew a fist back and punched Mee Noi square in the face. Blood spurted from the man's nose, and he let out a small cry. Rex immediately backed up to the door. He felt it bump against his back as someone tried to get in to respond to the cry. But he was more than a match for the slightly-built assistant, so the door would open only an inch.

Over his shoulder, he said, "No worries, just a small accident. The undersecretary just bumped into something —all is good here. Nothing to worry about."

His assurances must have satisfied the assistant, who stopped trying to open the door. Rex leaned back and closed it all the way, then locked it.

Meanwhile, Mee Noi had snatched a handkerchief out of his suit pocket and staunched the flow of blood. "You'll pay dearly for that," he snarled.

Narong answered, "I don't think you understand the situation. If you don't tell me where my sister is immediately, I have a good mind to pitch you out that window. Your assistant is cheaply bought. No one will ever know why you decided to jump out the window."

Mee Noi deflated like a pricked balloon. "Wait. There's no need for violence. I do not know where your sister is, but Ritthirong Kachonpadunkitti may. Go and ask him. And by the way, I have no interest in your father's land."

"I know you're lying. If my sister is harmed, I will return to finish this," Narong threatened. "And if Ritthirong has been warned before we get to him, I'll do the same."

"I promise," Mee Noi stuttered. "I have nothing to do with this, and I've forgotten Ritthirong's number."

"I'm sure your assistant will have it."

Narong nodded once, gave Mee Noi another stern look backed up by shaking his fist in the man's face, and turned toward the door. Rex kept an eye on Mee Noi, in case he had a weapon in the desk. When Narong reached him, he flipped the lock on the door and opened it, backing out in Narong's wake after Digger also went through.

On the way out, they got the telephone number and

address for Ritthirong Kachonpadunkitti from the very cooperative assistant.

Downstairs, Rex asked if Narong knew Ritthirong.

"Yes. He is one of my patients, in fact. Mee Noi was lying when he said he wasn't part of this. Ritthirong is a mercenary, not a politician. If he's involved, my sister is in physical danger, and you were right all along. He would have no compunction in having his own sick fun with her before killing her, whether or not my father complies with the demands."

Without commenting on Narong's medical practice and how he knew so much about a dubious patient, Rex let Digger into the car and got in himself. They'd been using Narong's car, since he knew his way around the city. Now he headed northwest, toward an area where the tsunami of 2004 had taken thousands of lives. Rex kept to himself the worry that loss of life had happened again only yesterday, or the day before. He wasn't certain, so much had happened since the sirens woke him.

Another half hour of driving brought them to the outskirts of a populous area almost due north and across a bay from the village where Sunstra's parents' beach house had been. Though it was only about nine miles from the center of Phuket according to Rex's mapping app on his cellphone, the roads didn't go directly there, but meandered as if they'd been laid out by a young puppy. Their drive along the coast was hindered by detours around low areas where the tsunami had left floodwaters trapped by higher land between them and the sea.

By the time they arrived in Naka Thani Village, Narong was nearly crazy with his worry about what was happening to Sunstra. He was driving recklessly enough that Rex felt the need to warn him to slow down within the village, before he killed a pedestrian.

"I can't," Narong muttered. "What if he…"

To distract him and get an idea of what they were walking into, Rex asked Narong how he knew of Ritthirong and his status as a mercenary.

"I have a lot of ex-military patients," Narong answered. "Because I'm ex-military myself, they come to me from all over Phuket Island, and even beyond. Some have injuries from skirmishes or from training accidents that have lifelong consequences. For some, I'm a sympathetic shoulder to unburden themselves of bitterness and resentments they still carry from their military service. Ritthirong is unusual in that respect. He is not bitter or resentful, but he lost a foot to a training accident, and the stump occasionally needs care."

"I don't understand," Rex said. "He's disabled, but still a mercenary?"

"I said he lost a foot, not that he is disabled. He does not let it stop him. And I know of his occupation because he brags about it. Because of doctor-patient confidentiality, I cannot report him to authorities."

Rex thought for a moment, then said, "So he's not just a thug. He's a hit-man, with military training, and a cunning one at that."

"Precisely. Let me repeat my warning to you. Don't get in my way. If he attacks us, stay back, so I can defend myself, and you by extension."

Rex nodded. "Just one favor. I know you're anxious about Sunstra, and so am I. But Digger needs a run, and I think we need some planning. Pull over."

"No, there's no time."

"Listen. You admitted I was right before. Stop now. The

dog needs a break and we need a plan. You can't just storm in there half-cocked."

Narong reluctantly agreed and pulled over next to a park, under the shade of a large tree. They all got out of the car, and Rex took Digger off the leash so he could have a runabout and do his thing. While they waited for him to come back, Narong took up his argument again.

"I don't know what plans you think we can make. I'm going to knock on the door and gain entrance with some ruse. You stay outside."

Rex began by placating Narong. "I stayed out of the way at the undersecretary's office, didn't I?"

"You did well, and it was helpful when you kept the assistant out of the office. But this is an entirely different matter. You could be badly hurt. I can't have you distracting me. I will have my hands full and won't be able to rescue you. This is about my sister. In fact, I think it would be better if I leave you and your dog here while I take care of matters."

Rex had just about enough of Narong's arrogance. It was obvious Narong was not thinking clearly. There was nothing wrong with healthy confidence. But the way Narong was acting, he was about to get himself and maybe Sunstra killed.

It was time to set Narong straight.

Rex looked Narong in the eyes and spoke soft and measuredly. "No, I won't stay outside, and I won't be left here. I can help, and I will. Get over it."

Rex expected an argument. What he didn't expect was for Narong to take a swipe at him with a closed fist. He parried it automatically, and the fight was on.

If Narong was surprised at a 'disabled' man knowing how to fight, he didn't show it. It soon became clear he was a Muay Thai master. Without missing a beat when Rex countered his punch, Narong twisted at the hips and came up with a vicious knee aimed straight for Rex's jaw. Rex twisted out of the way, grabbed the knee and pushed back. He didn't want to injure Narong, although he could have done so with ease. His goal was only to stop his senseless aggression. By the sounds of it, to take on Ritthirong they'd both need to be in top physical condition.

From the corner of his eye, Rex saw Digger charging and yelled, "Stop!" Digger took a few more steps before coming to a stop. Rex was fully engaged with Narong, who hadn't reacted to the command, recovered from Rex's push, and moved in again.

This time, he was more cautious and didn't try to kick at Rex. Rex's parries were lightning-quick, and maybe Narong had enough reason operating to know he'd end up on his back if he used his feet again. Instead, he protected his face and head with raised arms and approached in a boxer stance.

Rex's fighting style used a blend of techniques from the various martial arts at which he was an expert. If he'd needed to disable Narong, he would've used Krav Maga. The philosophy of which was to disable an opponent with force as quickly and efficiently as possible—even pre-emptively. Rex was ruthlessly effective at it, and he could have killed Narong in less than a minute if that had been his mission. But it wasn't.

Rex's Tai Chi expertise was a more effective method for what he had in mind. Its philosophy was more or less the exact opposite of Krav Maga, which was to stop aggression and not to disable the opponent.

Eventually, after Rex had dodged, parried or ducked all of what Narong threw at him, and receiving a few light blows from Rex in the process, Narong dropped his arms and stepped back.

As if they'd been engaging in a formal sparring match at a dojo, he bowed in Rex's direction—with a stupefied look on his face.

Rex returned the gesture.

Narong, still befuddled, spoke first. "You are not what you seemed." He used a quiet, calm tone. Gone was the arrogance and anger he'd spoken with before. If he wasn't exactly humble, at least he was no longer cocky.

Rex extended his hand, an invitation to shake hands with a worthy opponent. Narong took it firmly. "I think you'd better tell me who and what you are."

Chapter Nineteen

"That's not relevant to our situation," Rex answered. "In fact, if you ever talk about this or what we do next, we'll have another fight, and then I won't hold back."

The intense stare from Rex's dark eyes that accompanied those words apparently convinced Narong to swear to secrecy. "I won't. Believe me. Tell me this, though. Are you a tactical expert?"

"Among other things," Rex answered calmly. "Now, shall we get down to business? We need to reconnoiter before we go barging in like raging bulls and get Sunstra killed. Once we know who is in the house, where they're deployed, and what kind of firepower they have, *then* we can plan how to get in."

"Okay. But… what if she's not there?"

"Narong listen to yourself! For a man with such high education and specialist military training, you ask stupid questions. Stop thinking about the what ifs until we have established the facts."

"But… What if they don't agree to give proof of life?"

"Didn't you listen to what I just said? Well, if you really want to know, and I hate to say it, Narong, but the only reason to refuse is if they can't. If they've already killed…"

"Stop! I can't hear that. Let's do it your way, and may your Christian God help you if the delay costs her life."

"Narong, I thought we'd settled this. Your threats do nothing but annoy me, and we don't have time for that. Let's go."

With an uneasy truce established and Digger keeping a wary watch on them, they got back into the car and approached the address where Ritthirong lived.

Rex was unconvinced they'd hold Sunstra there, but it was the only lead they had.

He had Narong park about a block away.

"How will we discover everything you want to know?" Narong asked.

"We're going to watch the house for the rest of the day, and then I'm going to send Digger in closer for a look inside."

"But what help will that be? He can't tell you what he sees!"

"Just trust me. He's also not what he seems, and you aren't to talk about that, either."

By now, Narong was thoroughly confused about his companions, but he had enough time to compose himself and enough reason to relent and go with what Rex suggested.

"All right. How do you want to watch the house?"

"I'm going to find some place where I can watch the back and the grounds. You get a little closer in the car, but try to pick a place where you won't be observed. Watch the front, make a note of who comes and who goes, whether they're carrying anything out or in, whatever you see, and report it to me. Give me your cell phone number. And by the way, silence the ringer. We don't want to call attention to you if someone from the house happens to be passing by. I'll do the same."

Rex would have paid a lot of money to have the same kind of comms setup he had with Digger. However, he neither had any spare equipment for a human nor the time to go and buy it. He had only Digger's night rig in the back-pack he'd left the house with. They'd need it in an hour or so when it got dark.

He was making himself comfortable in a tree that over-looked Ritthirong's back yard when he felt his phone vibrate. He answered and said "Go," very quietly.

Narong's voice came through. "I just heard from my father. The kidnappers have agreed to provide proof of life. He managed to get them to agree to bring it to him in person. They're going to meet him in Bangkok in three hours."

"Great. There's the first item to take off your worry-list," Rex answered.

He reckoned the proof would be emailed to a co-conspirator, to be printed out and then hand-delivered to Sunstra's father. Or it would be put on a private plane soon. Either way, now that he knew Sunstra was alive right now, he was confident of getting her out safely—if she was in the house in front of him. Nevertheless, there was no time to waste.

He mentally urged the sun to set sooner, knowing the most reliable information would come from Digger's recon-naissance, not from watching the house.

The time passed slowly when one had to wait. During his training and in the years that followed on missions, Rex had learned that the life of a black ops field operator was one of endless traveling from one location to another, followed by extended spells of mind-numbing tedium, punctuated by bursts of absolute violence and terror.

And then there was the waiting. Waiting for the target or a contact to turn up, waiting for the target to make a move, waiting for someone to complete a task before the next one could begin, waiting for the right time, waiting for the sun to set so he could send Digger in to gather the information he needed.

It took a strong kind of psyche not to go crazy from all the waiting. For some of the experienced operators, this waiting was a terrible time as they were visited by the night-mares of their previous missions—the people they'd killed, the times when they were almost killed... Those were the times when hate for the enemy and what they did came to the forefront, but during their training they were taught to get rid of the emotions of hate.

"Don't hate them – it will kill you. Instead kill them, so they can't kill again," was the refrain the instructors played in their heads when hate wanted to take possession of them.

Rex didn't hate those who took Sunstra, but he was singularly pissed with them.

Digger was getting restless, accustomed now to being fed at regular intervals. Rex thought about how he could return both himself and the dog to peak mission condition when this was all over. It gave him something to take his mind off what could be happening in the house until they had a clear picture.

When at last it was too dark for him to see Digger concealed in the garden surrounding the tree, Rex slipped out of his hiding place and put Digger's gear on. He put the comms unit in Digger's ear first.

"It's time to work, boy."

Digger's ears perked up, and Rex felt the dog's heart beat faster and stronger under his hands as he buckled the harness and affixed the night-vision camera.

He bent down, took Digger's face in his hands, and pushed his nose lightly against the dog's wet nose and said, "Good boy! You love to work, don't you? We'll do more of that, I promise. Now, scout!"

Digger took off in a flash in the direction Rex pointed, toward the next house over, Ritthirong's. He ran silently and with purpose. Rex returned to his position in the tree to watch and direct Digger right and left based on what the camera was showing him on his iPad. In doing so, he had Digger work his way to a window that was half-hidden by shrubbery.

"Look inside, boy." he directed.

Digger rose until the camera was pointed inside the house. The room beyond was empty of everything but the furniture that revealed it was a dining room.

No good.

"Good boy. Hide and scout." Rex had discovered by accident that the dog was intelligent enough to understand compound commands Rex made up from the single commands he knew, even commands that seemed incompatible.

Though Digger's original owner and trainer, Rex's deceased friend Trevor, had used mostly one-word commands, there had been a few Rex heard him use that were compound ones, like Close Hide, Quiet Attack, Circle and Return, Go Right or Go Left that led him to believe he could combine some. Digger knew Hide and Scout meant be extra cautious to remain unseen while scouting.

It was only later that Rex, through studying books and internet information, learned the simpler, one-word commands were most easily understood by military dogs. He reckoned Digger was a genius among his peers.

Digger was at the next window and immediately positioned himself so that the camera pointed inside, reconfirming Rex's opinion of his intelligence.

This room had two humans in it, one of which was Ritthirong, Rex thought, based on Narong's description. Next to the slightly-built Thai man standing next to him, Ritthirong looked like a sumo wrestler. Rex whistled softly. The guy was big. He wouldn't be an easy take-down, and if he had martial arts training, which Rex assumed he did because of his military training, he was going to be formidable.

Going by the looks, the guy next to him would be easier to take down, though. He wasn't as big as Narong, and he had an air of deference to Ritthirong that indicated he was an underling, maybe even a servant.

"Got it, Digger. Good boy. Hide and scout."

The picture jostled as Digger went to the next window.

Pay dirt!

Sunstra was there, sitting cross-legged on a bed, her arms bound behind her back, and a dim lamp burning on the bedside table next to her. Rex's heart twisted. Had she been like that for three days now? How were they feeding her, if they were? Had they given her arms any relief from the awkward position now and then? It was difficult to tell in the low light, which as dim as it was still interfered with the night-vision camera. Rex couldn't see her expression.

Is she without hope? Is she crying?

The good news was that one swipe of a sharp knife, or a twist of handcuff keys, depending on what was binding her wrists, should free her to run. She was facing the window, but Rex assumed she wasn't seeing Digger, who would have been in full view if he hadn't blended with the night. He wished there was something he could do to alert her that help was coming.

Digger must have recognized her because he let out a soft whine which Rex could hear in his earphones.

"Good boy! Thank you. I saw her. Hide and scout." Rex heard another quiet whine. Digger's instinct would have been to go to her right then, just as Rex wanted to do but knew it was not the time yet.

It's a good thing Narong is not here to see this. He would have been running to break through the window by now.

Digger's training was strong enough to make him obey, leave her window, and move stealthily to the next one. That room was completely dark.

Rex visualized the size of the room based on the previous one, Sunstra's prison. There could be two, maybe as many as four more guards in that room, if there were bunk beds. Most likely two, he thought. Two others would be somewhere else in the house, but Digger's reconnaissance didn't show them.

Would have been nice to have had an infrared body-heat sensor rigged to Digger so I could've detected any people in there.

Rex's sense of geometry told him there were interior rooms, maybe a couple. A kitchen, which he hadn't seen in the camera, and probably at least one bathroom. Two rooms into which even the night vision camera didn't penetrate, including the one next to Sunstra's. The house wasn't much bigger, he reckoned. Maybe one more room, or a storage space, that didn't have a window.

At most, six people inside, not counting Sunstra. Including one mountain of a mercenary.

Piece of cake.

He called Digger back to his location and then called Narong on his cell phone.

"I've seen Sunstra. She's in the room to the left of the entrance, and there's no one with her. There's a big bruiser of a man in the room to the right of the entrance, I take it that's Ritthirong, and a small man, maybe a servant, in there with him. I reckon four more guards at most, and two are probably sleeping.

"As soon as Digger gets back here, I'll make my way to the front door, bust it in, and take care of the big dude and whoever is with him. You come in right behind me and go for Sunstra. Her arms are bound behind her back, but her feet aren't shackled. Just hustle her up and out, and we'll free her arms when it's all over. Got all that?"

Narong took the time to express his relief that Sunstra appeared to be okay. Then he raised a practical question.

"What about the other guards?"

"I'll deal with them after I deal with the big guy."

"Probably. But you're talking about taking on six men, including one of the most lethal mercenaries in Thailand. As soon as I have Sunstra safe in the car, I'll come and help."

"That might be helpful, but your first priority is Sunstra. Got it?"

"Yes."

"Now, wait for my count and then come in at speed."

Rex dropped out of the tree to meet Digger, who'd just arrived. He quickly relieved him of the harness and gear and said, "Ready boy? Quiet attack!"

He took off with Digger keeping pace at his side, vaulted the low wall that separated Ritthirong's house from its neighbor whose tree he'd been hiding in, and charged the door. One mighty kick sent it crashing into the wall next to it, and Rex was through. He turned right at the first door and caught Ritthirong running toward him. Not more than two seconds had passed since the noise of the door being kicked in had rung through the house.

Digger went for the servant, leaping on him and taking him down. The man's head hit the floor with a thud and he went limp. Then the dog turned to help Rex, correctly sensing that the small man was not a threat anymore. Rex was using every trick in his arsenal to attack Ritthirong before the man could bring his own to bear. But the mountainous man was as unstoppable as a speeding train. He was making progress toward the door, evidently intent on getting to Sunstra while the minor impediment of Rex pounding on him to get him to stop only slightly hindered his movements.

Rex could only hope Narong had followed his instruction and acted quickly. The noise would surely have roused the sleeping guards, and those on duty would arrive at any moment. He had to disable Ritthirong before they got there, or he would soon be outnumbered and overpowered.

He got the big man's neck in a chokehold, but it was like trying to choke a bull. It barely slowed him down. Suddenly, Ritthirong let out a bellow like the bull he was imitating. Rex didn't have time to look, it was Digger playing his part in it. He used his left fist to deliver a blow to the Thai's kidney, then had to let go of the chokehold as a massive elbow swung his way.

He barely had time to take note that Digger was indeed fastened to Ritthirong's left calf like a leech, growling and viciously twisting and turning his head to inflict maximum damage to the muscle.

Rex was about to wade in with another take-down attempt when he sensed movement behind him. He whirled with a Muay Thai kick and caught a new actor in the melee in the neck, felling him instantly.

That was when he turned his attention to the door and saw another newcomer charging toward him. He brought down the leg that had kicked the guy in the neck, shifting his weight to it and immediately bringing the other leg up. The roundhouse didn't have time to reach its full power, but it was enough to stagger the newcomer.

He swung his elbow back with every foot-pound of strength he had, catching Ritthirong in the liver, but in the process Ritthirong got hold of his arm and twisted, sending Rex to the floor in a flip. While he was down there, Rex punched the littlest guy in the throat to ensure he'd stay out of the fight, then rotated in a move worthy of a master break-dancer to reinforce the kicks he'd given to the two guards, and finally rolled out of the way of Ritthirong's size twelve foot, which was aimed at his throat in a nasty attempt to stomp him.

Rex sprang to his feet, arms up in defense, and took stock of the situation. No one else had charged in within the last thirty seconds, but he had three adversaries, including one that could crush the life out of him if he got hold of him.

Movement past the door caught his attention. He caught sight of a bare, feminine foot trailing the body it belonged to, and close behind, Narong for a split second framed by the door.

Then he had to execute another combination move to counter the two guards, who'd recovered far too quickly. He knocked one out with a haymaker while kicking the other away. Ritthirong had recovered enough from the liver punch and tried to charge, but then Digger let go of his one mangled calf and went for the back of the other knee, which brought the brute to his knees, howling in rage.

Ritthirong turned, swinging wildly at the dog, but Digger darted in, snapped at the flailing arms, and dodged back out of reach. Rex reckoned he had time to take the remaining standing guard out of the picture, if the others didn't charge in from the doorway. No sooner had he thought it, then a new man did appear at the door, but he quickly went down, revealing Narong behind him, who was already fighting with a second newcomer.

Check, it's over.

Rex knocked out the guard he'd been fighting, and grabbed a heavy-looking vase, which he brought down with all his might on the crown of Ritthirong's head. Ritthirong's eyes turned in their sockets, but he took forever to fall over, like a giant sequoia finally giving up the ghost. He was well and truly knocked out— down for the count when Rex checked.

With his three taken care of, he turned to help Narong. However, it wasn't necessary. Narong had both the late-comer guards down, one unconscious and the other nursing a broken arm.

Rex stood wearily and sighed.

Narong had a wide grin when he said, "What took you so long? I thought you'd surely have them all knocked out and trussed like roasting chickens by the time I got back."

Rex grinned back and good-naturedly gave him a middle finger in response.

"Let's get them secured."

After checking that Sunstra was not in physical distress, Rex and Narong took their time in the house, arranging matters so the police would not have to make guesses about what had happened and why, when they got there.

Two hours later, some fifteen minutes after Narong's anonymous call to the local police, he, Sunstra, Digger, and Rex were nowhere in the vicinity when the police arrived.

The four of them were at a restaurant on the other side of town, enjoying a late-night supper, including a whole roast chicken for Digger.

At Ritthirong's home, police found the front door wide open and everyone inside tied up, two to a room behind locked interior doors. Police had long known of Ritthirong's skullduggery, but they hadn't been able to get sufficient evidence to move the corrupt judiciary in the town to issue a warrant for his arrest. They found plenty in a neatly-formatted report in the living room on a low table, weighted down with a remnant of a heavy ceramic vase with gold trim.

In one of the bedrooms, of which there were three, they found the man himself, sporting a knot on his head the size of an orange and in a vicious mood. They wisely left him tied up while they explored the rest of the house. The most surprising thing they found was the assistant of the under-secretary of Mining and Development, who claimed he was only there at the behest of his employer. He was supposed to hand-carry a warning message to Ritthirong, but he'd been too late. When he got there, the attackers were just wrapping things up.

"No, I'm sorry. I don't know who they were. I've never seen them before," he claimed.

The officer knew the assistant was lying, but for now there were more important things to do.

"What will you tell your employer?" one officer asked.

"I'm handing in my resignation in the morning," he

said, his eyes big as saucers. "I never signed up for this. This kind of job hazard is not for me."

So, they let him go but told him he'd have to make himself available for further questioning and a statement later on.

A call went through to the Phuket police, who picked up the undersecretary and charged him with numerous crimes based on the information Ritthirong gave them, corroboration from the four guards and one other man, who turned out to be Ritthirong's business manager. The typed report was inadmissible, of course. Not because it was obtained under duress, because it wasn't, but the person who wrote it was unknown. However, it provided sufficient probable cause to open extensive investigations.

———

Due to the nature of Thailand's 'forgive and forget' culture, neither Rex nor the siblings had much faith that any of the conspirators would receive more than a slap on the wrist.

Thailand's history was rife with examples of leaders at the top of the food chain being ousted only to rise in favor again within a few years.

However, even if the land again became a magnet for corrupt officials, they thought Sunstra would be safe from harm. The story of the thrashing Ritthirong had received would surely cause his "business" to fail and give anyone with similar ideas reason to reconsider getting involved.

Chapter Twenty

Kraisee had returned to his own apartment, to make room for Sunstra and Rex at Narong's three-bedroom house. Narong had booked a hotel suite for his parents, who were to arrive the next day.

On the morning after the rescue, Sunstra was still resting when Rex made his appearance in the kitchen. Narong had summoned Kraisee back to cater the breakfast meal for his sister and Rex, and the brothers were deep in conversation regarding the lavish meal to be prepared in celebration of Sunstra's rescue and thanksgiving to Rex and Digger for their help.

As Rex entered the room, he caught a fragment of conversation about their debt of gratitude for his help. Rex was not a person who liked to be in the limelight. What he overheard made him feel a bit self-conscious. He felt that he would have been obligated to help Sunstra and her family just because of the injustice that was being done to them. To make them aware of his presence, he gave a polite cough as he entered.

To his surprise, both men put their palms together in a prayer-like pose, touched their chins with their fingertips, and gave a slight bow.

"What's this?" he asked, automatically returning the gesture but not understanding why they'd done it.

"Respect," Narong answered in English. "With your help I was able to keep my promise to my family," he continued, cutting his eyes toward Kraisee and then back to Rex. "My brother and my parents know that you and your dog were of assistance to me in rescuing my sister. We are grateful."

Rex understood Narong's remark about his promise to mean he hadn't detailed exactly how Rex and Digger had been of assistance. He nodded his understanding. "I was happy to help in any small way."

Narong spoke in rapid Thai to Kraisee and then led Rex into the dining room, where they both took seats a moment before Kraisee followed with cups of fragrant coffee laced with condensed milk. Rex was surprised to find how much he liked it, since he usually took his coffee black. Kraisee went back to the kitchen, while Narong gave Rex an overview of how the day would proceed.

"I will pick up my parents at the airport shortly after our noon meal. While we, Sunstra, Kraisee, and I, are modern, and don't stand on ceremony much, my parents are traditional." He stopped talking and took a sip of his coffee, as if unsure how to proceed.

Rex understood the hesitation. It would be very rude to blatantly instruct a guest on the rules of etiquette, and yet Narong wanted him to make a good impression on the older Chevapravatgumrongs. Fortunately, Sunstra and his class in Thai language had taught him the basics. As a younger person, even though a guest, he would be expected to perform the *wai*, the gesture with which Narong and Kraisee had greeted him a few minutes before, when he met them. Depending on how the older couple viewed his status compared to theirs, they might return it.

"Don't worry, *Khun* Narong," Rex said, deliberately placing a light emphasis on the universal word for Mister, Missus, or Miss to show that he understood the proper form of address. "I will try my best not to embarrass you. Perhaps you could tell me your parents' names, so I may address them correctly?"

He didn't know why surnames were reserved for formal occasions or written documents, but he suspected it had to do with the odd rule Sunstra had told him about weeks before. It wasn't surprising that pronunciation of the long names might be awkward, given that they had nothing to do with the language really, but were adopted only a few decades before. That was his theory, at least. Maybe he'd have time to ask Sunstra later.

"My father's name is Kasem, and my mother's is Nin. Thank you for asking."

It was a matter of curiosity for Rex that he and Narong, with whom he'd had an uneasy and even testy relationship the previous day, were now behaving as politely as they did. Since Narong had set the precedent, however, it was incumbent on him to maintain the veneer. At least it was more comfortable than always having to balance between deferring to Narong's mild arrogance and displaying some machismo of his own.

"If you will excuse me, I must give Digger a chance to get outside for a bit of exercise. Do I have time before breakfast?"

"Yes, of course. I will inform Kraisee. And then I will

check on my sister to see how she's doing and if she will join us."

Rex took Digger on his leash around the neighborhood, stopping at every tree and shrub in which Digger displayed a particular interest this morning. About an hour later, they arrived back at Narong's house. Rex stopped and was debating whether he should knock when the front door swung open and Sunstra emerged, looking like a dark-haired angel. It made Rex's breath catch in his throat. However, he waited for her to make the first move.

For the first time since they'd become closer than merely teacher and student, Sunstra's enthusiastic hug didn't draw a disapproving growl from Digger. In fact, while enjoying holding her slim body, Rex was aware of Digger's tail thumping against the back of his legs. After a moment that was a little too short for Rex's preference, Sunstra let go and stepped back.

"I cannot thank you enough," she said.

Rex smiled gently. "Hey, I thought we got past that last night. It was nothing."

"It wasn't nothing, Ruan. You saved my life." She took his hand and led him into the house. "You should see the feast Kraisee is preparing for tonight. My parents will be here this afternoon, and we will have a proper celebration in your honor."

"No, Sunstra, I only helped your brother. Narong was the one who saved you."

Sunstra fixed him with a hard stare. "Ruan, I know my brother well. He is capable, but he is a hothead. Against that killer, he would have been completely out of his depth. He'd have gotten himself killed, and I would have been killed as well.

"I don't know where and how you got the skills I've seen

before and again last night when I caught a glimpse of you handling that monster Ritthirong by yourself as Narong got me to safety."

"Sunstra…"

"Don't worry. I won't give away your secret. But you must accept my gratitude."

With that, she stepped forward and kissed him hard on the lips. This time, Digger growled.

"Oh, be quiet, Digger. It's just gratitude, not an attempt to seduce your precious Ruan." Sunstra laughed as she bent and roughed up Digger's ears, to his evident delight, as he relaxed into a wide grin and leaned against her legs. "Thank you, too, Digger! I know you helped. I saw you biting that bad man."

Digger's tail wagged harder. Rex glanced down at him with a mixture of pleasure and irritation.

What a brown-noser!

Narong came to the door then and told them Kraisee had breakfast ready.

That afternoon, Rex had some time to himself with Digger as Kraisee was closeted in the kitchen and Sunstra had accompanied Narong to the airport to pick up their parents. He took the opportunity to take Digger outside into the gardens in the back for a run and a bit of training.

Rex was pleased that Digger hadn't lost his edge when they were in working mode. He easily climbed a tree to the roof of Narong's house, and he executed the commands Rex gave with no hesitation. Rex's worry that Digger had lost some of his skill through their neglect of training time was dispelled. He remembered Trevor telling him that with the military dogs, the ones who got selected for training, the handlers had to show them something only three times and the dogs would forever remember it.

When they went inside, Kraisee had set snacks of every imaginable kind on low tables in what Rex was calling the living room, for lack of a better term. The seating was arranged for comfortable conversation, though the furniture was a bit low for Rex's height. His knees stuck up at a comical angle when he was seated, but if the furniture had been higher, Sunstra's feet would have dangled above the floor.

Shortly afterward, Sunstra's parents arrived. Rex gave the *wai* gesture to the parents, Kasem and Nin, who returned the gesture to Rex in the midst of smiles all around.

Then Sunstra began laughing.

Kasem smiled indulgently. "Let us dispense with this formality. Khun Ruan, thank you from the bottom of our hearts for our daughter's safe return to us. And thank you for helping us keep our land. We are most grateful."

Once more, Rex explained that it was Narong who'd rescued Sunstra, with only a little help from him, which he was glad to give. It was beginning to feel natural to spin the story that way, so when the old couple turned beaming faces on their eldest son in approval, Rex was happy to not be the center of attention anymore.

Narong, however, looked a bit uncomfortable. Only a slight shake of Rex's head made him remember his promise and press his lips together, so he didn't reveal just how much Rex had 'helped'.

"It was my honor to save my sister," he said, his head bowed modestly.

Kasem clapped his hands. "Then, let us celebrate!

Khun Ruan, you are in for a treat. My son Kraisee is an amazing talent in the kitchen."

Rex answered, "Please, it is just Ruan. Your daughter is a special friend, the best teacher I ever had, and I think of your sons as my friends as well."

Everyone except Kraisee went into the living room and began snacking. And of course, among all the jubilation, Digger made sure he was the center of attention much of the time. Fortunately, he didn't embarrass Rex and demonstrated his class by not clowning for them. Instead, every now and then when in need of attention, he walked sedately to each person and accepted pats and treats before lying down next to Rex's chair.

Rex let the others guide the conversation. He was surprised they didn't discuss the kidnapping. Instead, the family focused on him and his impressions of Thailand. Naturally, when Kraisee joined them after seeing to the progress of the meal, the subject turned to food.

As they were speaking in Thai during that conversation, Rex was a little confused when someone mentioned their forebears had been 'food growers'. It took him a moment to remember that the words for rice and food were identical. They'd been rice farmers when the family's land had been farmed. Even though Kasem had become a physician, he still had a great deal of respect for the land and the farmers, which was natural considering he was a practicing Buddhist from a northern province where Chinese influence was great. As such, he honored his parents and ancestors, as did Narong, on a family shrine that Kraisee had pointed out to Rex when he first arrived.

One day I'll take up the study of comparative religions. It's a natural adjunct to the study of history.

Rex didn't consider himself religious, but he respected

the religious beliefs of others. But that didn't stop him from thinking that it might be interesting to do a comparative study of the world's main religions.

But as the conversation swirled around him, Rex had to give up those private thoughts and pay close attention to follow what everyone was saying in Thai. He was not fluent enough yet to follow a rapid exchange among the family members.

Later, his right hand deftly gathering sticky rice in a ball and dipping it into Kraisee's fabulous sauces, Rex found himself the subject of amusement again.

"You are welcome to use a fork in the way of your people," Narong had said. "We will not be offended."

"But this is so much more fun," Rex said, grinning. "The only problem is, at home I'd lick my fingers."

"You can always ask Digger to lick them for you." Sunstra giggled.

The family exploded in laughter. Rex hadn't been part of a family for most of his adult life, and he was now thoroughly enjoying the experience. They'd made him comfortable enough that he wasn't self-conscious about etiquette.

The feast lasted late into the night, and when Kasem and Nin finally left, Rex fell into bed thinking he'd had enough rice in various incarnations, all of it delicious, to last him at least a month.

Chapter Twenty-One

Sunstra was already a couple of days late returning to work, but her ordeal was enough of an excuse for the delay. However, although her manager had been kind enough to allow her the time off, she was now needed in the classroom, and they were urging her to return.

Sunstra agreed. She realized that getting back into the teaching routine would keep her mind off the horrific experience of being abducted and threatened with death.

Rex had seen enough of Phuket for the time being, and besides, he wanted to keep an eye on Sunstra and make sure she was recovering mentally and emotionally. They flew back to Bangkok together.

On the flight back, Sunstra seemed distracted, but each time he asked her if she was all right, she smiled and said yes. After the third time, she put her hand on his arm.

"Ruan, please. I'm fine. I'm just working through an important matter, and your concern is distracting me."

Rex apologized and fell silent and into his own thoughts about the future.

When they landed, Rex insisted on delivering her to her door in the taxi he'd hired. When she protested, he played the Narong card.

"Your brother would skin me alive if he found out I just sent you on your way, unprotected in the big city." He kept his face straight, knowing the way he'd put it would needle her, but began to smirk as she proved him correct.

"My brother does not control my life, Ruan Daniel, and neither do you. I lived in this big city long before I…" She stopped short, having noticed the smirk. She laughed and lightly struck his arm with a delicate fist. "Oh, you're teasing. Well, I'll have something to say to my brother, anyway."

"Please don't. He said nothing of the kind to me. He trusts your judgment. I was just kidding. You've been so serious, I wanted to lighten your mood."

She laughed again. "Well, I have something very serious to think about. Thank you for seeing me home, Ruan."

"Dinner later?" he asked.

"Maybe tomorrow. Call me." With that, she dismissed him, climbed out of the taxi, and hefted her own luggage without a backward glance.

It gave him only a slight pang. He should have at least carried her bag in for her, but she hadn't given him a chance. Digger mirrored his confusion with a small whine as he watched her walk away.

Rex gave the driver his address, and they left the curb.

"Hey, buddy. I thought you didn't want us together," Rex said to the dog.

Digger was watching the sights outside the taxi, but his ears pricked up when he heard Rex's alternate appellation for him. He turned at 'buddy' and let his grin show. His tail thumped once, indicating to Rex that he'd heard the remark but didn't understand it or was not going to honor it with a reply. Rex gave up trying to understand the dog's motivation.

Maybe Sunstra had been right when she said Digger was trying to save her from me. He seems to like her as long as we're not in physical contact.

Arriving back at his apartment after a week on Phuket Island, Rex discovered his pantry was bare. Since Sunstra had declined dinner, he ordered in and turned in early, enjoying a good night's sleep for the first time since being awakened by emergency sirens.

The next day, he waited until he knew Sunstra would be home from her first day back at school, and then he called her. She answered after one ring.

"Hi, Ruan."

"Hey. How was school?"

"It was good. It took my mind off things. I have made my decision."

"What decision?" he asked.

"I'll tell you at dinner, if the invitation is still open."

"You know it is. Shall I pick you up around seven?"

"No, I'll meet you." Sunstra named a restaurant they'd enjoyed before and told him to make it eight.

"I'll see you there," he replied.

He had nearly seven hours to wait, and the curiosity was driving him mad, so he took Digger and a Frisbee he'd found at a street market and went out for a bit of fun in a nearby park.

Digger loved it.

Rex remembered he'd intended to get both of them back on their training regimen, so he put Digger through a few of his paces, just those that wouldn't alarm passers-by.

After several hours, it was time to go and get ready for what he suspected would be his last date with Sunstra. A little melancholy settled in when he thought about it, but not as much as it would have been a couple of weeks before. He was already moving on from Thailand in his heart and mind.

At eight, having left Digger with the Kong full of a special treat of roast duck and peanut butter—something he himself would have found repulsive but which Digger lived for and considered a reward for a job well done—Rex presented himself at the restaurant. Sunstra was there before him. She waved to get his attention, and he joined her at the secluded table.

"Thank you for coming, Ruan," she said.

Suddenly, he had the idea that this was more of a formal meeting that she'd orchestrated than a dinner date. Unused to such a situation, he sat down without speaking and turned his intense dark eyes on hers with focused attention.

She nodded. "Let's order, and then I'll tell you what I've been thinking about since yesterday."

"Sounds like a plan," he said, caution in his tone.

"Shall I order for you?" she asked.

"Please do," he responded, sensing the occasion demanded some measure of formality. He didn't often find himself off-balance, but the air of portent was palpable.

Sunstra ordered quickly and confidently in Thai. Rex caught a few of the familiar dishes and knew others to be items he hadn't tried before.

This is going to be an adventurous meal, if nothing else.

When at last the server left the area, he leaned forward.

He was about to ask her what all the mystery was, when she gently laid the tips of her fingers on his lips.

"Please. Let me speak. Then you can ask questions."

Rex sat back in his chair and nodded. "All right. It seems this is your show. Go for it."

She smiled. "I love your Americanisms. Yes, I know you are supposedly British, but I have learned to spot the differences in my job. Don't bother to deny it. My brother has spoken of some mysterious competencies you have that were instrumental in my rescue, though he wouldn't tell me what they are. He said something about he'd tell me, but then you might kill him? I assume he was joking."

Rex stayed silent, although he let a hint of a grin settle on his face. He hadn't actually threatened to kill her brother, but he was glad Narong was keeping his word and being circumspect with the details of the rescue, as he'd promised.

Sunstra had paused to leave room for his comment, but when he didn't make one, she went on.

"We have never had reason to speak of it, but I do have a university degree. I prepared myself for a post in government. You didn't know that."

Rex's raised eyebrows were the only encouragement she needed to go on.

"I once thought I'd like a job in our foreign service. Accordingly, I studied what you might call political arts?"

"Political science," he corrected.

"Just so. In any case, when I completed my studies, my father was already in conflict with some officials in government who wanted his land. It didn't seem to be a possibility for me to get a post, so I went into teaching."

Rex nodded. Her ambitions had mirrored his youthful ones. He understood the pain of giving them up, though her reasons weren't as traumatic as his had been. "Go on."

"I have realized that was a cowardly decision," she blurted. "I am going to run for election on an anti-corruption platform. There. I've said it out loud for the first time. *That* is my decision."

Rex's jaw dropped. If she'd said she'd decided to emigrate to Tierra del Fuego or become the first Thai astronaut, he wouldn't have been more surprised.

"Are you serious? You've just endured three days of captivity and threats to your life, because of politicians, and you're going to openly defy the powers that be? What does your family say about this?"

She tilted her little pointed chin and frowned. "They do not know. They might not like it, but they won't stop me. I am an independent woman, and I make my own decisions."

Rex risked her wrath by making another protest. "Sunstra, do you have any idea how brutal a political race could be? These people aren't moral or ethical. They could do any number of things to make your life miserable. Drag your name through the mud, so you'd never get another job again if you fail to win your race, for example. You must have the support of your family, if nothing else. Think of the expense!"

"Ruan, I am not naïve. That's why I had to spend so much time thinking it through. But my mind is made up. I'm doing it, with or without the support of my family. I do expect their support, though. I think my father will be proud."

Rex sincerely hoped so. Having met her father, he admired the man's dignity and his commitment to his principles. Sunstra knew her father better than he did, of course. If she thought he would support her decision, he probably would. Her older brother might be a different story, but it was her business.

He extended his hand across the table, and she shook it

firmly. "In that case," he intoned, "may I be the first to congratulate you on a bold decision."

She smiled and released his hand. "Thank you, Ruan. I knew you'd understand. That means a lot to me."

Rex smiled and said, "When you are elected to office and need a bodyguard, just let me know. Digger and I will be honored."

"I might just take your number." She laughed.

They made small talk after that until their food came, and then they were silent as they enjoyed it. As Rex was spooning the last of the sweet and sticky rice dessert into his mouth, Sunstra brought the subject back to mind.

"Elections will be held soon. I must begin my campaign immediately. Though I won't have much free time, you are welcome to stay and see what happens. Maybe even campaign for me?" She chuckled. "I'd definitely like to continue our friendship, if you feel the same way."

"That goes without saying, Sunstra. My philosophy about friendship is that a friendship that comes to an end has never been friendship to start with."

"I like that. Those are wise words, Ruan. I might just use that in one of my campaign speeches."

"You're welcome. Just don't tell the people they're my words. Like you, I also have other plans, and it's time to move on with them. I'll watch for news of you, though. I'll be hoping to call you with congratulations in a few months."

"As you wish," she said, with another heart-stopping smile. Her beautiful eyes sparkled with life and anticipation. "I'll miss you and Digger, but I'll probably be too busy to pine much."

Rex laughed. "Indeed."

He snatched the check before she could, though she

reached for it. "Let me," he said. "My small contribution to your campaign."

As they left the restaurant to go their separate ways, Rex bent to kiss her chastely on the cheek. "I'll never forget you, Sunstra Chevapravatgumrong. You're a wonderful person that'll make someone more deserving than me very happy one day."

"Nor will I forget you, Ruan Daniel."

Chapter Twenty-Two

Bangkok had lost its long-term appeal for Rex. He'd seen the historic sites, experienced the cuisine, learned a new close-combat technique and a new language, and had many massages. It was time to leave.

Before he left Thailand, however, he wanted to collect the stories of at least some of the seven major Hill Tribes who resided in the mountainous north of Thailand. These people were living a sort of shadow existence. Unrecognized as citizens, they were nevertheless left alone by the Thai government. They were refugees from neighboring countries, including China, Tibet, and Myanmar who'd migrated to Thailand over the past two-hundred years.

Retaining their own languages, styles of art and dress, indeed, their entire culture except where tourism had modified it, these people were shy but as hospitable as the Thai people in general. Rex though it would be remiss of him not to collect their history from oral tradition while he was still in Thailand.

Rex contacted Sunstra and donated the tuk-tuk to her

for her campaign. She didn't want to take it, but he was very persuasive and told her how much she and her staff were going to need it. In the end she accepted and gave him a kiss on the cheek, which Digger didn't object to.

With the tuk-tuk donated for a good cause, he traveled with Digger by bus and extended thumb to one of the villages. He'd finished with that village, representative of its tribe, and was on the way to another when his secured satellite phone rang.

Rehka's voice on the other end was full of excitement. "Ruan, I have done it! I have access to Mutaib's and Usama's offshore accounts! Now I need your direction for what to do with them."

Rex reflected that he'd chosen well in deciding to employ Rehka. He was certain she was scrupulously honest. He never spared one moment on the thought that she could easily take the money for herself and disappear with her whole family. It didn't hurt that she owed him her freedom, but even so, he had trusted her, and she had just confirmed that she had the skill and the integrity to do what he needed and then wait for his directions.

"Ruan? Are you still there?"

"Oh, sorry, Rehka. Had something on my mind. That's really great news. So, I think it would be best if I return to Mumbai, and we'll work through it together. I'll see you as soon as I can get a flight. You okay with that?"

"Why do you even ask? I can't wait to see you."

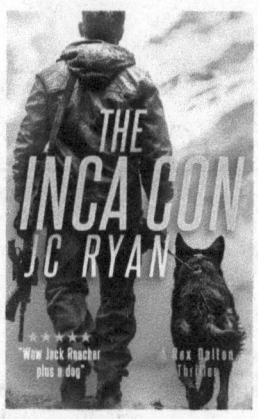

www.vinci-books.com/inca-con

In the Andes, a sinister plot threatens an archaeological dream.

When Rex Dalton joins an expedition to a remote Andean village, he discovers that the investors are victims of a sophisticated and sinister con. With time running out, he and Digger are pitted against criminal masterminds that will stop at nothing to protect their interests.

Turn the page for a free preview…

The Inca Con: Chapter One

He'd chosen the high road, which added two hours to his route, but he was in no hurry. The roundabout route rewarded him with a lifetime of breathtaking vistas to this invigorating experience. Walking easterly from Abancay to Curahuasi, Peru, the higher peaks of the Andes were usually on his left, while glimpses through river gorges flanked by lower peaks could be had on the right. Plenty of switchbacks reversed the views in some places, and at times they walked toward the north or the south, following the steep road that would eventually lead downward as steeply as it had led upward.

Rex Dalton and his constant companion, his Dutch Shepherd dog, Digger, had arrived in Lima on the day of the spring equinox. In the intervening weeks, they'd wandered as the wind took them, exploring the rich history of the western bulge of Peru. They had just missed the best traveling weather for one of the most famous of all Peruvian destinations, Machu Picchu. Before the rainy season started in earnest, it was time.

Approaching the Sacred Valley on foot had been a whim, but after nearly fifteen hours on the road from Abancay, where he turned in his rental vehicle, Rex was committed to the plan. The difference between fifteen hours on foot and four in a car was the opportunity to stop and drink in the spectacular scenery that would have otherwise whizzed by barely noticed.

Digger seemed to enjoy it, too, dashing here and there to inspect some item of interest only to a dog. A bit of a nuisance, but a bit entertaining, was Digger's apparent mission to catch a vizcacha. The peculiar animals, related to chinchillas but looking more like a long-tailed, rather short-eared rabbit, were plentiful along the trail. Their homes, resembling a prairie-dog colony in numbers, interested Digger a great deal, and Rex found it amusing to see him race around after an adult, while the rest of them hurried the babies in among the rocks where he couldn't reach them.

Rex had camped overnight, though he could have walked the entire fifteen hours in one day. He'd elected to break it up because there would be only twelve hours of sunlight. Starting before dawn wouldn't have been an issue but descending the last set of switchbacks after dark wasn't prudent. He planned to get to Curahuasi in time for a midday meal before finding a room for the night, and he was on target when he reached the intersection of Route 116 – the high road – and 3S, the main road. Only a little over a mile to go.

When Rex arrived in the center of the dusty little town, he looked for a café first. He'd have preferred one with tables outside, but the first one he came to had only a wide opening for a door, with tables inside. Oddly enough, it was a pizza restaurant. Digger's nose lifted at the aromas emanating from the open door.

"Really, Digger? You want pizza in Peru?"

Digger's mouth stretched in a dog's broad grin, his tongue lolled out, and if he could have spoken, he'd have said, "Why not?"

Rex could think of several reasons why not, including that garlic, an essential ingredient of pizza in his opinion, was toxic to dogs. And the fact that he had no idea what a Peruvian pizza might have for toppings. But it seemed to be the only option. He'd have to figure out something else for Digger, who had made it clear from the time they became partners that he expected human food. They'd had an ongoing struggle on that subject, and Rex had become an expert on what Digger could or shouldn't eat.

As he stepped inside, and his eyes adjusted to the dim interior from the bright sunlight outside, he realized it wasn't the dingy, dirt-floored establishment he'd expected. The tables were draped with cream-colored cloths, brown runners placed precisely in the middle to bisect the length. A clean tile floor, devoid of animal hair, suggested the place wasn't dog-friendly.

"Digger, you'd better wait outside. Stay."

Digger flopped down on his belly with a sigh that Rex interpreted as dissatisfied acquiescence.

"Hey, you picked the place. I'll bring you a slice, and if you behave, maybe more."

Rex went on in and allowed a young woman with a sleek black bun at the nape of her neck to lead him to a table. The establishment wasn't crowded, but a couple of other tables were occupied, one by two men talking earnestly in stage whispers, and the other by an older couple, tanned and fit for their apparent age, which was betrayed by their graying hair.

The two men could have been American or European, but they spoke English. The whispers didn't convey an accent. Both were blond, though one was older than the other. Rex couldn't see their eyes, and they didn't appear to be much above or below average height.

Rex ordered the house special, wondering if it would resemble an American or an Italian pizza in any way. He didn't particularly care. He wasn't picky about his food. In his thirty-six years, he'd dined on unremarkable but satisfying home cooking from the German-influenced kitchen of his midwestern-raised mother, to the cuisine of countries all over the world in his past life as a field operative of a top-secret black ops paramilitary organization. It was during his time in the latter that he learned that food, as long as it wouldn't make him sick, was fuel, which would keep him going.

Digger might turn up his nose, though. He was a real pain in the ass sometimes when it came to food.

As he waited for his order to arrive, Rex became aware that the two men were discussing a misfortune that had befallen one of them, the younger one. He would have ignored them but couldn't tune them out as the whispers became more strident and the younger man's voice rose. With less than a foot between the tables, which were lined up in military precision, side by side, he and the couple on the other side of the table where the men were seated were witnesses to the narrative, whether they wanted to hear it or not.

"I'm telling you, I don't know what to do," the younger man hissed.

"And I'm telling you, your money is gone, and you might as well accept that fact," the older one said with exaggerated patience. "There's nothing you *can* do. Unless you've left something out. Tell me again."

The younger man sighed heavily. "Telling you again won't change the outcome." His voice raised a few decibels.

"Just humor me."

"Okay. Now please pay attention. I was looking at some curios in the marketplace over in Abancay. They looked old, and I thought I'd buy a statue of Virachocha."

The older man interrupted. "Who's that again?"

"The Inca god of creation. I've told you this. And it isn't important. Just that it looked old." The younger man was becoming more agitated, and his voice was rising in both volume and pitch.

"Okay, go on."

"So, I'm looking at this statue, and this woman comes up to me and takes it out of my hands. She says, 'It's a fake.'"

"Did you believe her?"

"For crap's sake, will you just let me tell the story?"

The older man took a long drink from the brown bottle in front of him and slammed it back on the table. "Fine. Go ahead."

"I asked her, 'How do you know?', and she says she's Ministry. She hands me a card. Ministry of Culture, it says. She tells me there are more fakes being sold than the genuine article, and then, get this, she says, 'Lucky for you. Because it's illegal to buy or sell the genuine antiquities.'

"It freaked me out. It was like she was threatening me, just because I was looking at this old statue, you know? Like she was accusing me of robbing Peru's cultural heritage."

He stopped speaking, shook his head, and took a swig from his bottle of beer.

"And that was the last you saw her?"

"Yeah, that was the last I saw her. But before she left, she told me to call the number on her card if anyone offered me something that could be original. Seems the shop owners have gotten smart. They don't put the real antiquities out for people to see. But when they see an American, like me, they think we all have money."

"You do have money."

"That's beside the point. They'll offer the real deal to Americans or other unsuspecting tourists. So, I was supposed to call this Agent Gonzales if that happened to me, and she'd come and arrest the shop owner."

"And it happened to you," the older man prompted, earning a glare from the raconteur.

"It did. Very next day, I'm looking at stuff in the Mercado Central here, and this creepy old man comes out and whispers he has what I'm looking for in the back. I mean, could have been anything, from drugs to women, whatever. I was curious, right? So, I follow him into the back room, and there's this gorgeous gold medallion, had to be a good four ounces of high-grade gold, right? Carved in the shape of Inti."

"I hesitate to ask."

"The sun god. Jeez, don't you ever listen to anything I tell you?"

The older man made a gesture with his hand, to indicate the other should continue.

"So, I'm thinking, that's gotta be the genuine article. I tell the shop owner, 'Just a minute. I need to get my partner here to talk about this.' I'm gonna call the agent, right?

Gonzales? But the shop owner says, 'You must hurry. Another buyer is coming.'

"I figure he's playing me, but then someone else comes in to look at it. He and the shop owner are jabbering away in Spanish, and he pulls out his wallet. So I figure, I've got seconds to get this, and I'd better do it, or this priceless artifact will be gone forever. You should have seen the guy who entered the shop – he was swarthy."

"Swarthy? Did you just say 'swarthy'? The hell does that mean?"

"You know. Dark. Dark skin, dark hair, dark personality. I figure he's a smuggler."

"Oh, for Pete's sake." The older guy shook his head.

Rex shared his disgust. The young guy was looking more and more like an idiot. He couldn't help but think about the old adage; since light travels faster than sound, some people appear to be bright until you hear them speak. He'd just described every native Peruvian male, except for the personality part. Rex thought Peruvians were unaccountably happy, considering their poverty.

"No, seriously. This guy was not a good guy. So I tell the shop owner I'll take it."

"You bought the statue."

"Yeah, but first it was a bidding war. I had to pay almost a hundred thousand for it."

"Dollars?" The older man's eyebrows levitated to a spot under his shock of blond bangs.

"Soles. But that's still a chunk of change, about thirty K US, right?"

"And you bought it why?"

"To keep it from leaving the country, of course! I figured the shop owner would get busted, I'd get my money back, and this Gonzales chick might be grateful, know what I mean?" The younger man leered as he said it.

"Shit, Junior, how thick are you? So, what's the problem? She's not grateful enough?"

"The *problem* is that the number on the card is fake."

"And…"

"And as soon as I called and found out it was fake, I got worried. I mean, could I get arrested for buying this thing?"

"I have no idea, you might very well find your ass in the slammer."

"Well, *that's* my problem."

"I suggest you pre-empt it all and go to the police and tell *them* this story," the older man said, with a show of indifference.

"Dude, that could get me thrown in jail!" the young man continued.

"I don't know what you want me to do about it. I swear you've got more money than brains. Man up."

"But, Uncle Rich, what if they arrest me?"

Rex looked from the blond older man to the tow-headed youth. He didn't see a resemblance, other than the color of their hair. Maybe the 'uncle' was honorary.

What difference does it make? None. I'm not involved in this.

Rex had to put his hand over his face to hide the grin when Einstein's words popped up in his mind. "Two things are infinite: the universe and human stupidity; and I'm not sure about the universe."

Rex had eaten all the pizza he wanted, and he knew Digger was waiting for his share. Surprisingly, it was a pretty good pizza. Digger would be picky about it. He didn't like green peppers. But he'd eat everything else, including the olives. For some unknown reason, Digger loved black olives.

The pepperoni was a given, but the pepperoni here had garlic in it. He asked the server to have a small pizza made up with no sauce, cheese, or pepperoni. "Just vegetables, please, but no garlic, onions or green pepper. And lots of grilled chicken." Digger would enjoy it, it wouldn't be bad for him, and it would help extend the supply of dog food they could carry while on foot.

Without waiting to hear the uncle's solution to the kid's problem, Rex left the café and gave Digger his 'pizza'. Rex still found it bewildering to watch the dog every time he fed him. A meal which Rex would spend twenty to thirty minutes on to consume, Digger gulped down in less than thirty seconds with three to four bites, and then, most amazing of all, he would sit back, lick his lips, and look accusatory at Rex as if to say, 'when are you going to feed me? I had nothing to eat all day'.

When the dog had finished, Rex rooted in Digger's pannier-style backpack for his collapsible bowl and a bottle of water. Digger lapped the water gratefully.

When Rex had first planned to hike instead of driving in Peru, he'd wondered if Digger would allow the contraption. He needn't have worried. It was like the harness Digger was used to, except that it had a soft cotton canvas bridge over his back with expandable side pockets attached. A sturdy handle allowed him to hold it while Digger stepped out when it was time to take it off, and provided a ring for a leash, which stayed in one of the pockets most of the time.

Rex had put it on him empty at first. When Digger didn't seem to mind that, he started adding weight gradually, until the dog was carrying his own food, water, and toys. At the last minute, Rex had added the coms units and night-vision camera that fit on Digger's regular harness. He didn't anticipate trouble, but experience had taught him trouble seemed to find them anyway. In any case, Rex thought it was only fair for Digger to carry his share, and Digger seemed to agree.

The next order of business was a room, a shower, and a good night's sleep in a real bed. Then he'd replenish their supplies and be on his way to Cuzco.

The Inca Con: Chapter Two

The next destination on Rex's agenda was Cusco, jumping off point for tourist attractions throughout the Sacred Valley. Rex wasn't averse to using a guide, and in some cases, it was required. However, walking in a crowd of tourists wasn't his style. Besides, he preferred to acclimate himself to the altitude gradually, by walking from village to village and the historical sites that fascinated him.

Rex had a keen interest in history. Formally trained with double major undergraduate degrees in history and linguistics, he'd further refined his interests with an MA in political science. He had a facility with languages that bordered on the savant. He would have described it, had anyone asked, as a 'knack', but that would have been modesty—it was much more than that. He'd been fluent in German, French and Spanish by the time he'd graduated high school and had a little Italian then, as well. Since then he'd become fluent in Italian and added Mandarin, Arabic, and Hindi to his language repertoire. On this trip, within a couple of months of arriving in Peru, he'd been conversant in

Quechuan, the ancient language spoken by eight to ten million of the indigenous people living in the more isolated rural areas across South America, including Peru.

However, he'd abandoned his plans to enter diplomatic service after his parents and younger siblings, a brother and a sister, were killed in the 2004 bombing of a train station in Madrid, where the family was enjoying a vacation in celebration of Rex's newly-minted MA. A short stint in the Marines followed by training as a Delta Force operator, rapidly morphed into his being headhunted as a special field operative for Crisis Response Consultancy, otherwise known as CRC after the fashion of government alphabet-soup agencies. CRC operated where the government, including the CIA, could not.

All that and more was water under the bridge now. Circumstances beyond his control had interrupted that career, and his control of circumstances since then was what had given him the leisure to pursue his first love – the study of history – in the places where it had happened. He had no specific itinerary, no timelines to keep—he went where he wanted when he wanted, and Digger never protested. For now, that was Peru and the Inca civilization.

How he'd come to be traveling with Digger, the former Australian military dog, was part of the career interruption. He'd become a reluctant dog owner with the dying words of a good friend, Digger's handler. In the months since then, Rex had overcome his childhood fear of dogs and learned to trust Digger's instincts, though, especially in the early days of their friendship, he wasn't always fond of the dog's demands. In his field agent days at CRC, Rex preferred to work alone on missions, but since he and Digger were forced to team up, he had to admit, Digger was smarter than many people. The dog had snatched Rex's bacon out of the fire as often as it had been the other way around. They'd wrangled for alpha position in the early days, and Rex had a sneaking suspicion that if he held it, it was only because Digger had conceded out of pity or because Rex had bribed him with peanut butter served in his favorite toy, a now-battered Kong, the peculiar-looking, ribbed, hard-rubber toy dogs loved because of its erratic way of bouncing and the hole in the middle that could hide treats. Digger preferred his filled with peanut butter or lamb jerky. Truth be told, they probably shared the alpha position depending on the circumstances.

On the morning after his arrival in Curahuasi, refreshed by a tepid shower and a night's sleep in a real, though lumpy, bed, Rex was whistling cheerily as he and Digger stopped at a bodega for supplies to last for the three-day trek to Cusco. His map had estimated twenty-eight hours of walking. He'd decided to take it leisurely, making sure he'd be able to see the sights along the way, even if that required a side-trek. Once he reached Cusco, he'd turn north for the Sacred Valley, and take the adventures as they came.

At the bodega, he recognized the older couple who'd been seated on the other side of the men who'd had such a contentious conversation at the pizza restaurant the evening before. He avoided eye contact, unwilling to be delayed by chatting with them, though they seemed pleasant enough.

However, they must have taken note of him as he had of them. The woman greeted him in English. Rex, ever mindful of not standing out, smiled just politely enough to avoid rudeness and returned her greeting with the same careful degree of civility. Then he turned away, intent on his shopping. It didn't work.

"Excuse me, young man, but weren't you in the restaurant last night? We didn't get a chance to introduce

ourselves, because of that... oh dear how shall I say it...
'unfortunate' young man."

Rex looked around, pretending he thought she was
talking to someone else.

"Yes, I'm sure it was you. Tell me, what did you think of
that story we couldn't help but overhear?"

He had to give her credit for her persistence. "I didn't
pay much attention," he responded.

"You left before the end of it. But we could see you were
paying attention. Oh, I'm sorry, how rude of me. I'm
Florence Marks. Barry! Barry, come over here and meet...
I'm sorry, what did you say your name was?"

"I didn't say." Rex had several names, as evidenced by
his growing collection of passports. He was traveling under
the name Raymond Davis for this trip. Resigned to the
delay, he answered, "Ray Davis. Nice to meet you."

"And you. So, what did you think of that?" she
continued.

Rex glanced at Mr. Marks, who offered him a weak
smile in apology for his wife's insistence on engaging Rex in
conversation.

Rex decided to be honest, and hope that would help
extricate him from the conversation sooner. "I think he was
scammed and should go to the police. But honestly, it's none
of my business."

"That's exactly what we told him! Isn't it, dear?" She
included her silent husband as if it mattered to Rex whether
he agreed or not. The man didn't respond.

"Good advice. Hope he took it," Rex muttered.

"Oh, is that your furbaby?" Mrs. Marks exclaimed,
spotting Digger's interest from just outside the open-air
market's entrance.

Rex suppressed an urge to roll his eyes.

Good thing Digger wouldn't understand that word or Mrs. Marks might have earned herself an indignant growl.

"Well, I call him my buddy," he managed. Digger's tail wagged uncertainly, as if he understood he was being discussed.

"May I pet him?"

"He's a working dog, ma'am. Whether you can pet him depends on him. He'll let you know if it's okay."

Mrs. Marks' face went blank. "Oh, well, then I probably shouldn't."

"Maybe that's best. If you'll excuse me, I meant to get an early start. I just need to finish my shopping. Goodbye." Rex edged away, hoping he hadn't sounded too abrupt, but there was probably not an easy way to make a clean getaway from Mrs. Marks.

"We're going to Cusco. Is that where you're headed?"

Rex would have preferred not to say, but he didn't have a ready lie. "Er, yes."

"Maybe we'll see you there at dinner. Are you taking the Machu Picchu tour that starts day after tomorrow?"

"No, ma'am. I'm hiking. I won't be there until the day after that. To Cusco, I mean." Rex took another step away before Mrs. Marks squealed in dismay.

"I'm so sorry! Maybe we could give you a lift to Cusco? Would that help?"

Before Rex could think of a polite way to say he was walking by choice and wouldn't accept a lift even if she weren't a nosy old biddy, Mr. Marks finally intervened.

"Dear, maybe Mr. Davis is walking because he wants to." To Rex, he said, "I'm sorry. Since our son died, she thinks she needs to mother anyone his age."

Rex felt instant regret about his thoughts on the woman's gregariousness. Having lost his entire family, he understood lingering grief and that it manifested in different ways at different times. "That's all right. I'm sorry for your loss."

"It was a long time ago. But thank you." Mr. Marks stuck out his hand and Rex shook it firmly. "Good luck on your hike."

"Thanks. Good luck on your tour."

Rex finished his shopping, spoke in Quechuan to the proprietor as he paid for his purchases, and waved at the Marks couple as he left. Mrs. Marks gave him a fond smile and waved back.

Before they left, Rex divided his purchases among his backpack and the panniers on Digger's, then hoisted his to his back. "Let's hit the trail, buddy."

Despite it being late spring south of the equator, the air was chilly at nearly nine-thousand feet of altitude. Rex was dressed for the temperature he expected at noon, around fifty-six degrees. At only a couple of hours after sunrise, he'd donned a colorful poncho against the chill. Earlier in his travels, he'd abandoned his light jacket for the poncho. It was much more practical, as it served double duty as a blanket at night and was more efficiently folded for carrying in a roll on his backpack when he was ready to take it off. Otherwise, he wore long denim pants, a Western-style long-sleeved plaid shirt with snaps, and a pair of light-weight hiking boots.

Except for the high-end ultralight backpack he wore, the hiking boots, and his stature, just under six feet but taller than the natives by inches, he might have passed for an urban Peruvian. Weeks in the high altitude of Peru had tanned his naturally olive skin to a shade close to the Mestizo population of the cities, and his dark hair and eyes did nothing to dispel that image. Even his Quechuan, limited though it was, sounded native, an indication of his rare talent for picking up languages and speaking them without a foreign accent. And his vocabulary was growing with every encounter he had with the native population. He'd be fluent before he left, if the past was anything to go by.

Digger showed his appreciation for the cool of the early morning by trotting up to twenty or thirty yards ahead and then racing back to Rex's side. He'd be less eager to run ahead when the sun was directly overhead, beating on his black coat with the intensity found only where the air was thinner. Fortunately, their path crossed streams and lay under trees in many spots, when it wasn't along well-populated areas in the rich farmland of the region. Digger would have plenty of water or shade to stay cool enough, and their trek would gain over two thousand feet of altitude, making it cooler yet. And another reason to hike rather than drive was that they'd get used to the altitude gradually, as they'd been doing since leaving Lima.

Rex let his mind wander, relaxing his guard for the first time since he'd begun to suspect that his old mentor, John Brandt, CEO of CRC, was looking for him. No one would look for him here.

The Inca Con: Chapter Three

Flo Marks was seventy-three, but she prided herself on having the health and body of a much younger woman and thought of herself as middle aged. Unlike her husband, she didn't take her identity from the company he'd sold a few years before. She had her own independent persona with a lot of interests, health and fitness among them. She hadn't allowed herself to get soft or fat... *heavy*, she reminded herself. Political correctness was important to her, too. She had to admit, though, she was glad the trail from Cusco to Machu Picchu led mostly downward. More for Barry's sake than hers.

Flo worried about Barry. Before he'd retired, he worked too hard and neglected his health. Afterward, he'd seemed lost, bereft of his beloved company. Their only son, dead too young from a motorcycle accident, had left them without the pleasure of grandchildren in their old age. She missed him, and she missed the grandchildren they'd never have. So, when Barry found a new interest and suggested they spend some of the fortune he'd made from the sale of the company by encouraging responsible archaeology, she'd welcomed it as a worthy cause which would serve a dual purpose—a new interest that would keep her husband's mind occupied and get him out of the house.

They'd set aside an amount that would see them comfortably through the rest of their lives, enough to take trips like this one and stay busy. And the rest, Barry had placed in a foundation for grants to archaeologists. Flo knew he hoped a find of historic significance would come of it before they died. Which, if it depended on her, she intended to be no less than twenty-five or thirty years from now, because she took care of her health and tried to take care of Barry's, though he didn't seem to appreciate it.

She turned to gaze fondly at her tall husband, still handsome, though his red hair had turned white.

"What?" he asked after becoming aware she was staring at him.

"Do you need more sunscreen?" she asked.

"Stop fussing, Flo. I'm fine."

She looked away to hide a smile. He knew she adored him. She knew the feeling was mutual. They'd been married long enough that neither needed to say it every time they thought it.

They'd walked another half a mile when Flo noticed someone was pacing them. She looked to her left, and to her surprise, saw the young man from the restaurant in Curahuisa.

"Oh, hello," she said.

"Hi. I noticed you when we stopped for lunch. Didn't know you were taking this tour," he said.

Flo thought he left unsaid that he'd thought they were too old. She bristled a little.

"I wanted to thank you," he went on. "I took your advice and went to the police."

Flo's motherly instincts kicked in, though this young man was closer to the age a grandchild would have been, had her son lived. "Oh, I'm so glad! It worked out, I guess, since you're here."

"Well, I didn't get arrested. They laughed at me, though. I guess it's one of the oldest scams in the book. The woman who said she was from the Ministry of Culture, the shopkeeper, even the other customer, were probably all in on it."

The boy looked sheepish, Flo thought. She supposed she'd feel the same way, if she'd lost that much money. *Thirty-thousand dollars!*

"I hope that wasn't all you had," she said, inadvertently revealing she'd been eavesdropping on the details of his conversation with the older man.

"Oh, no. I mean, I can afford it, but no one likes to be scammed. And I should know better. By the way, I'm Junior Roper. Short for Walter Henry Roper Jr. You've probably heard of my dad."

Flo couldn't say she had, but she didn't want to embarrass the boy. "I'm sure I must have. But please forgive me, my memory…" She let it trail off. It went against her grain to admit to a failure of middle age, even as a polite fiction. She never, *ever*, thought of herself as elderly. Middle-aged was as far as she was willing to go.

"Anyway, I just wanted to thank you. I won't intrude on your holiday." He started to stride forward.

"Nonsense. We're on the same tour. How could you be intruding. Let me introduce you to my husband. Barry, do you remember this young man?"

She went on to remind him, and to introduce them.

Barry reached over to shake Junior's hand and say something vague and polite about Machu Picchu.

Junior's eyes lit up. "I've wanted all my life to see the ruins," he said. "I'm something of an amateur archaeologist."

Flo knew what would happen next. Before she fully articulated her thought, Barry had switched places with her to walk next to the young man. And before a minute had passed, the two were deep into a conversation about archaeology and the general lack of funding for it. Junior said he'd started to pursue it as a course of study leading to a career, but his father had needed his hand in the family business because of illness.

Hours later, Flo had begun to think of Junior as an orphan in need of a father figure, and her husband as the very man to fill the role. Between the rigors of business and their mutual love of archaeology, Barry and Junior had formed a fast bond.

Flo drifted away from the two to find someone else to talk with as they walked, and then found them still together when the group stopped for the night. As the porters pitched the tents and the cooks began preparing the meal, Junior excused himself.

"Did you enjoy your chat with the young man?" Flo asked Barry.

"I did, and it was more than a chat. You'll never guess what we talked about."

"Archaeology, obviously," she answered.

"Honey, he's done some digging around here…"

"As an archaeologist?" she interrupted.

"No, as in detecting. He's discovered ruins near a village high in the Andes, beyond Machu Picchu. No one knows about them. No tourists, I mean. And the ruins haven't been excavated. He's going there when this tour gets back to Cusco and get this… we're invited!"

Flo saw in Barry's face that he was completely in love with the idea of going. "How high?" she asked.

"Don't worry. Junior said we can take our time getting used to the altitude. And he'll bring oxygen for us, just in case."

"For you, you mean. I'll be fine." Flo patted Barry's protruding belly fondly. "Maybe this hike will help reduce that."

"We can go?" he asked, hopefully.

"My love, we can do anything you want," she answered. She was not going to spike his dreams.

Grab your copy…
www.vinci-books.com/inca-con

About the Author

JC Ryan is a bestselling author renowned for his intricate espionage, archaeological thrillers, and conspiracy mysteries. With over 30 acclaimed novels, including the popular Rex Dalton K9 Thrillers, Rossler Foundation Mysteries, and Carter Devereux Mystery Thrillers, Ryan has captivated readers around the globe.

Drawing from his diverse professional background—as a military officer, lawyer, and IT manager—Ryan creates compelling narratives that skillfully blend historical accuracy with thrilling adventure. He is celebrated as a master storyteller, known for crafting riveting plots, meticulous historical details, and engaging, multidimensional characters. Ryan's meticulous research lends authenticity and depth to each story, immersing readers in richly constructed worlds filled with intrigue, suspense, and adventure.

Fans of David Baldacci, Lee Child's Jack Reacher, Tom Clancy's Jack Ryan, Nelson DeMille's John Corey, Vince Flynn's Mitch Rapp, Mark Greaney's Gray Man, Gregg Hurwitz's Orphan X, Robert Ludlum's Jason Bourne, Daniel Silva's Gabriel Allon, Brad Taylor's Pike Logan, Brad Thor's Scot Harvath, James Rollins' Sigma Force, Steve Berry's Cotton Malone, and Dan Brown's Robert Langdon will find JC Ryan's novels equally compelling and unforgettable.

When not writing, Ryan enjoys spending time with his college sweetheart, whom he married in 1978. They are proud parents of two daughters, have two sons-in-law, and are grandparents to two grandchildren.